THE HIDDEN MAGIC OF ORDINARY THINGS

OLIVIA MCCULLOUGH

*To those who've always been the one others lean on, and to the love
that finally feels like rest.*

1

___

I could still taste this morning's ward spell, molasses and clove with an iron-sharp undertone—a whispered warning I'd grown accustomed to ignoring. It lingered on my tongue for hours after I gave the majority of my power to the stones in exchange for the valley's protection.

Charmwork was much more pleasant. Warm honey and cinnamon bloomed on my tongue each time I imbued enchantments, the sweetness a mask for the power coursing beneath.

I focused on the spray of white roses laid out before me, letting the honey-sweet taste of enchanting magic wash away the morning's ward work as I filled them with preservation magic to keep them fresh through tomorrow's ceremony.

Every morning this week, Sorcha had burst into my shop before the sun fully crested the Eastern mountain, checking on some detail or another. This was her third visit today, the little brass bell above the door still ringing when she gasped.

"Meira, the roses look perfect!" Sorcha made herself at home in the window seat behind my workbench and watched over my shoulder, her copper waves falling in her face when she leaned too close. "They'll stay fresh through the whole ceremony?"

"Through the ceremony and the celebration after," I promised. "Though they'll start to fade by the next morning."

Her enthusiasm filled every corner of the charm shop, like sunlight through a window. I loved seeing her so happy. Like all valley fae, her eyes shifted between amber and russet brown depending on her mood, and now they sparkled with each flash of magic, making even the simplest enchantments feel special with her wide-eyed wonder.

I'd grown used to working alone, but having my best friend fill my usually quiet shop with warmth and laughter made the magic flow easier through my fingers. Sorcha and I had shared everything since we were children: skinned knees and warm cinnamon buns, the harvest festival where she first danced with Conor, and the late night tears when I'd lost my parents.

"I can't believe I'm getting married tomorrow," Sorcha said, she looked both nervous and excited.

"Having second thoughts?" I teased.

"Gods, no." She laughed, but then grew quieter. "It's just... Conor's been so nervous about his ceremony speech. He keeps practicing it when he thinks I'm not listening, muttering to himself while he shaves."

I smiled, picturing steady, reliable Conor flustered over public speaking. "He'll be fine. You know he means every word."

"That's what makes him so nervous, I think," Sorcha said fondly. "He wants it to be perfect."

I couldn't help but smile, she was probably right. Conor, Sorcha, and I had all grown up in the valley together, and while he'd always been the quiet strength in our group, he showed his heart in small, constant ways. Like the way he'd casually scribble in his pocket notebook whenever Sorcha spoke of things she wanted, as if marking down mundane tasks instead of her dreams. Or how he traded his best catches with traveling merchants whenever they had something he knew would delight her.

Unlike other types of fae, our people weren't bound by magic to keep our promises, but Conor treated every word as if he were. If I even casually mentioned a problem when Conor was around, he'd show up at my door the next day, sleeves already rolled up to help.

That unwavering reliability was what made him perfect for Sorcha—his steady devotion grounding her wild spirit without trying to tame it.

There was a familiar knock at the back door, softer than you'd expect from someone built like a bear.

Calder let himself in, ducking through the frame like he had all week, and I barely looked up. At this point, my shop had become the unofficial drop site for wedding supplies, decorations, and whatever else Sorcha decided she needed last minute. Calder had delivered half of it.

He was Conor's best man, which meant I'd been seeing more of him lately than usual. Not that I was complaining. Sorcha had roped him into more errands than anyone should suffer in one week, it was a wonder he hadn't thrown her into the river.

She treated him like an older brother she could boss around, and he took it in stride the same way Conor did. Both males were steady, patient, and quietly protective underneath it all.

His movements were always quiet, yet deliberate. It seemed like someone his size should make more noise, but Calder never did. If his stature alone didn't mark him as forest fae, those golden-green eyes would've. Though his eyes held none of the wild danger I'd been warned about as a child.

He cleared his throat and glanced at Sorcha. "Brenna says —" He paused, already grimacing. "Brenna says to 'tell Sorcha the cream linen napkins are in the wardrobe behind the bar, and if she's changed her mind again, she can come dig them out for herself, because Brenna is done playing wedding.'"

He looked like he wanted to dissolve into the floor. Sorcha was entirely unfazed.

I bit back a smile. "Did she make you rehearse that before you could leave?"

"No. She wrote it down," he muttered, and waved a folded piece of paper.

"Speaking of the wedding," Sorcha's eyes glittered with mischief, having ignored Brenna's dig entirely, "I might have mentioned to the carpenter's son, Finn, that you don't have a date for the wedding tomorrow. You remember Finn, right? He seemed quite interested in catching up with you. And with each of you being unmarried—"

"Please don't start," I said, rolling my eyes.

"I just think the two of you would get along well if you'd give him a chance. I worry about you being lonely."

"I'm too busy to be lonely," I argued. "I wouldn't have time for a male even if I wanted one." Though, it wasn't entirely true.

Sorcha rolled her eyes. "Well, he's probably going to ask you to dance at the wedding," she said, "I don't even care who it's with, will you at least promise me you'll dance at some point during the night?"

I kept my head down, subtly blotting at the hint of blood in my nose, pretending to be interested in a non-existent scratch on my workbench. I was burning through too much magic, too quickly. Calder tried to muffle a laugh, but it was a low rumble he couldn't hide.

"I don't know what you think is so funny," I warned, "she'll find a date for you too." I regretted the words as soon as they left my mouth and wished I hadn't given her the idea.

Sorcha's face lit up. "Yes! Oh Calder, do you need a date for the wedding? Let me set you up if you don't already have one. Please?"

Calder looked from Sorcha to me, unsure if he wanted to bind himself in that commitment. Unlike valley fae, he would be bound to any promise he made, and also unlike us, forest fae couldn't lie.

"You wouldn't want to disappoint the bride, would you?" I asked, gleefully ensnaring him into the same trap I was in.

"Exactly Calder, you can't disappoint the bride. It's bad luck!" Sorcha said, while Calder rubbed the back of his neck, stressed. I grinned like a cat, pleased to have brought him down with me.

His face grew pink, the points of his ears tipped in red. Sorcha looked at him with all the hope of a child. I couldn't help the way my lips curled watching him flounder. This was the same fae who, after a particularly nasty storm, once lifted an ancient cedar that had fallen off of Farmer Tull's barn without breaking a sweat, while the rest of us could only stare as we looked on. Yet here he stood, brought low by the prospect of small talk and dancing. It shouldn't have been so endearing, and yet.

"Uh," Calder stalled as he looked around the shop, trying to find a way out of agreeing.

"You know what?" Sorcha clapped her hands together. "You two should just go together! You'll be there anyway. Plus, you already know each other, so you can just have fun instead of blind-date jitters. It's perfect!"

The suggestion hung in the air. Sorcha looked delighted, but I could feel heat creeping up my neck, and Calder had gone very still. I don't know if either of us was breathing.

"That's not—we don't—" I stammered.

"It's what the bride wants," Sorcha said innocently, though her grin was anything but.

I kept my eyes firmly anywhere that was not Calder.

Sorcha gathered her things to leave, practically dancing towards the door with the infectious joy of a bride-to-be. But just before she could get to the door, she stopped and turned to me, "Thank you again Meira, for preserving the flowers. I'll come by to pick them up as soon as you're finished?"

"I'll bring them by," I promised. "Should have them ready within the hour."

"Perfect. All of the lanterns are already set up in the meadow when you get there for the enchanting." She beamed, "You're the best."

Sorcha grinned from ear to ear as she left Calder and me alone in the shop.

As soon as the door shut completely behind her, I sighed and dropped my head into my hands.

"You forgot about the lanterns, didn't you?" Calder taunted, his eyes gleaming with pleasure.

"I'm a terrible friend," I groaned. I'd have to stay up all night to get them done between now and the wedding.

"You're not a terrible friend. You do seem like an over-booked friend to me," Calder observed quietly, his teasing tone replaced with concern. "Will you still have ward work to do in the morning?"

"I'll be alright," I promised, and I would. I always did, no matter what it cost me.

"Have you seen how many lanterns she has waiting for you out in that meadow? Enchanting all of them will be a lot of magic for one person," he said carefully. "Especially one person who has to work again in the morning. I'm heading back now to start setting up seating, I'd be happy to work on them with you if you wanted the help."

I looked up at him, surprised by the offer. After Sorcha's matchmaking ambush, I half expected him to flee the shop entirely.

"You don't have to," I said. "I think Sorcha just enjoys embarrassing me."

He huffed out a laugh. "Do you think I'm just offering to be polite?"

I glanced up at him, trying to read his expression. "Aren't you?"

"I'm many things, Meira, but I'm rarely polite for the sake of being polite."

It was the first time I remembered him saying my name, and I liked the way it sounded. But he had a point. From what I'd seen, Calder was always kind, but never disingenuous.

"So why are you offering to help then?"

"Because floating lantern enchantments are more taxing than they seem," he said. "And because you look like you haven't slept properly in weeks."

"I'm fine," I said on instinct, but the observation stung because it was true. I didn't let the words hit me though, I couldn't. If I acknowledged how worn down I was, my whole facade might crack.

"I'm sure you are, but the lantern enchantments will go faster with two people." He leaned against the doorframe. "Plus, if we pair off and work together tonight, Sorcha will be too pleased with herself to bother us with her other schemes."

"That's... actually brilliant."

"I have my moments," he said, shrugging. "So we're partners then?"

"Partners," I agreed. "For the lanterns."

"And the wedding?"

"You *did* make a great argument, and it seems like the practical thing to do. "

"Very practical," he agreed, and I caught the hint of a smile tugging at his mouth.

It made me smile too.

"I should finish these flowers first," I said, gesturing to the roses. "I'll meet you at the meadow in about an hour?"

"I'll be there."

After he left, I stood among the roses, trying to ignore the way my heart had picked up pace when he'd laughed. I told myself that it just made sense. Two people working to accomplish one task meant half the effort, surely. That flutter in my stomach was probably just relief at not having to do everything alone.

But as I tried to weave preservation charms through delicate petals, I couldn't stop thinking about how he'd said "I'm many things, Meira" and how much I wanted to know what those things were.

I pushed the thought away and focused on my work. I had flowers to finish and an evening of lantern enchanting ahead of me.

With Calder.

As partners.

If I weren't already late, I would've taken the long way to the meadow and walked along the river. But cutting through the village square was faster, if slightly more goat-infested.

Merchants were still packing up, spilling over every inch of cobblestone. The booths were crammed so tight I had to turn sideways to pass. Fabric snapped in the wind, herb bundles swung like charms overhead, and the same damn goat was wading through the fountain for the third time this week.

With the flowers in tow, I kept my head down, praying I wouldn't lock eyes with anyone still waiting on a charm order. I had no intention of slowing, but that was before I smelled the fresh baked cinnamon buns coming from Fern's bakery.

One stop wouldn't hurt. I would just take it with me, and eat it on my way there.

Fern's shop was small, and had only one table when she first opened, but that quickly changed when the number of loitering regulars outnumbered the available seats. There hadn't been an empty chair since, morning or night. Fern would say it made the place feel lively. I thought the lack of space made it harder to breathe.

"Afternoon, Meira" Fern said before I was fully inside. "What can I get for you? Your usual?"

"I think I'll have two today, I'll take one for Sorcha." She hadn't asked for anything, but if I knew Sorcha, she'd be so focused on getting every detail of the set up just right, she might not have eaten all day. It would do her good to have something on her stomach before a night of revelry.

"She'll love that," Fern said, boxing up two cinnamon buns.

I shrugged, paid her two silvers, and tucked the box under my arm . "She'd do the same for me." Nobody had ever surprised me with a cinnamon bun, actually. But I liked to think she would. If anyone ever did, it would be Sorcha.

Just as I was almost out the door, she called me back, "Oh Meira, I've been meaning to ask you to take a look at the weather-watch charm we got from you last month. It's acting strange. It says a storm's coming tomorrow, but the sky looks clear as crystal."

I stopped to examine the small weather charm hanging by her door. The enchanted raindrops inside the glass vial had turned a dark gray and swirled angrily. It looked like a storm in a bottle. I hoped it was wrong for Sorcha's sake.

"Probably just needs a refresh," I said, aiming to sound light-hearted, but hearing the rasp in my voice. No charm lasted forever, but I just made this one a few weeks ago. It shouldn't have run out so soon. And lately, even my most basic magic had started unraveling long before its time. "I'll stop by and fix it after the wedding. I can swing by next week, if that's okay?"

She nodded, her eyes kind. "No rush. We trust you, Meira."

I picked up my pace as I pushed my way through the market and headed for the meadow. At the edge of the village, just outside the tavern, I passed Nolan leaning against the stone wall, deep in conversation with his uncle, Elder Thomas, who stood rigid with his hands clasped behind his back. They both fell quiet when they saw me coming.

"Off to decorate for the wedding?" Nolan called, loud enough to draw attention. He grinned like we were friends. "Hope you've got enough magic in you to finish the job. Wouldn't want you to faint like the last time you looked this worn down."

I didn't slow my pace. "I haven't fainted in over two years, Nolan, it's amazing how much better I feel out from under your thumb."

His smile faltered for a moment before he recovered. It had been two years since I ended things. Long enough, apparently, for him to forget I wasn't as docile as he hoped I'd be.

"Of course," Elder Thomas said, his voice warm, but his gaze stayed on me too long. Like he was waiting for me to fail right then and there. "Though you do look a bit spent, Meira. It might be time the Council finds an appropriate partner for you. Someone to ease your burden."

I bristled.

The Council had always danced around it, luring me into a partnership with talk of support, shared duty, reinforcement for my magic—but this was the first time one of them had come close to saying it out loud.

Arranging a partner truly meant they were thinking of marrying me off.

I'd been dreading this since the very beginning, since the moment I stood in front of them in the chamber, a shell of my former self, and somehow convinced them to give me a chance on my own. A chance I nearly destroyed the first time I touched the wards.

And now, after everything, they were still circling.

It felt like failure to know it was at the forefront of their minds, that they were likely already discussing which eligible males in the village had both enough magic and enough patience to deal with me. I didn't imagine the list could be very long.

Because ward magic doesn't just require strength—it requires harmony and trust. It requires a bond that most only find through committed partnership, if at all.

The kind of deep, interwoven bond that only ever exists between those who've chosen each other completely. Though some throughout history, the unlucky few, had no say at all.

I could see Nolan's chest puffed up like a rooster out of the corner of my eye, like he was offering himself as a volunteer.

I refused to give him any of my attention.

I didn't stop walking. Just turned enough to toss a saccharine smile over my shoulder, threading venom into every word. "Thank you so much for the offer to help Elder Thomas, but I'm great."

Only when their voices faded behind me did I let my jaw unclench. I stole a breath and let my shoulders drop. I might be pushing myself too far, but I'd be damned if anger at Nolan pushed me over the edge.

My heart still thudded like I was preparing for a fight. The taste of iron that flooded my mouth told me I was halfway to losing.

2

———

Decorating for the ceremony was organized chaos, but I could see Sorcha's vision. At least a dozen people had busied themselves setting posts, hanging garlands, and arranging seating.

It looked like every spare piece of furniture in the village was sitting here in the meadow. Benches from the schoolhouse, stools from the tavern, chairs from the bakery—even old Hamish had wheeled his prized carved bench down from his front porch, though he'd made it clear only his grandchildren were allowed to sit on it.

Sorcha crossed the meadow barefoot, her rehearsal dress caught on the grass behind her and slowed her steps. She was flushed and windblown from the warm afternoon, but even so, she moved like she'd been born to command, snapping instructions as Conor and Calder followed like dutiful soldiers.

"No, that bench needs to face the arch!" she called to Conor, pointing with a bundle of ribbon. "And those flowers are drooping again!"

I tried to focus on the arch. On the flowers. On anything except the way Calder rolled up his sleeves and lifted one of the benches like it weighed nothing, arms flexing as he moved it into place. I tried not to notice the muscles across his back as he turned to change the bench's direction. Almost as hard as I tried not to turn back to look again.

It wasn't just his strength, it was the ease in how he carried himself. How naturally he fit in everywhere he went. He'd only lived in Glenmere for two years, but it seemed like the valley and everyone in it had just been waiting for him to show up.

It had taken me a long time to stop seeing him as the fae who found me collapsed in the grass. It took longer still to stop feeling humiliated every time I stood near him as if my magic might fail again just for old time's sake.

The day he arrived was also my first as the wardcrafter. My first day trying to prove I was strong enough, capable enough, anything enough to fill the space my parents left behind.

I'd promised Sorcha and Brenna I'd meet them for dinner at the tavern that night. I'd even smiled when I said it, sure that one successful solo renewal would be enough to convince them I was going to be okay.

When I didn't show up, they assumed I needed space.

No one knew I'd collapsed beside the northernmost ward-stone, face-down in the grass, blood crusting under my nose, and my magic dangerously close to being completely drained.

And then Calder Byrne walked into Glenmere.

A forest fae with no ties to the valley and no destination in mind, he wandered into Glenmere and happened upon my body, crumpled on the ground.

They told me later that he scooped me up—sword on his back, and a pack slung over one shoulder—and carried me straight down the cobblestone streets that led through the village square.

I woke up in his arms, with half the valley watching as he carried me to Aoife the healer's cottage. But the thing I remember most clearly was the feel of his heartbeat under my cheek.

Afterward, everyone would call him brave, gentle, and noble. And maybe, in another life, I could've looked at him with nothing but gratitude. But in this life, at that time, all I saw was proof that I could give every last part of myself, bleed myself dry for the people inside these wards, and it still wouldn't be enough.

But that was two years ago. Since then, I'd come to know him better—by proximity at first, through Conor and Sorcha, and eventually through the quiet, persistent way he showed up for people. He was kind and present in ways that had nothing to do with me.

Whatever resentment I'd carried softened over time, until all that remained was a kind of quiet understanding. Though we'd never spoken a word to each other about that day.

Now, I watched as he placed a bench, and when he noticed it wobbling, he crouched down and ran a hand along the frame. It looked like he just rubbed his hand over one of the legs. But when he stood and tested it again, the whole bench sat straighter.

He caught my eye over Sorcha's head as she directed him to move it three more inches to the left, and mouthed the words '*Save me*' with a look of such desperation that I had to bite my lip to keep from laughing.

"Meira!" Sorcha barreled over to me still barefoot. She had cinnamon icing on her chin, which I wiped away with my thumb in one quick, motherly motion. She barely reacted. We'd been taking care of each other like this since we were old enough to walk.

"Can you believe neither of those males said a damn thing?" she sighed, gesturing toward where Calder and Conor still worked. "Not about the frosting or the wilting flowers falling off of my head. Useless, both of them."

She shoved the crown toward me. "Can you fix it? It keeps dying no matter what I do."

I took it gently, careful not to jostle the failing enchantment. "Anything for you," I said dry as ever.

A shimmer of white fell like snow into my palms. I brushed it over the wilted blooms with the lightest touch, coaxing life back into each petal. A charm this small and delicate shouldn't have felt like work, but I'd used a lot of magic today.

"You're the best," Sorcha said, giving my arm a squeeze. Her voice softened. "Are you okay? You look—"

"I'm great," I said before she could finish her sentence, but Sorcha knew all of my tells.

She studied me for a moment, and then a sly grin spread across her face. "You sure you're not feeling a bit flustered with your date over there?"

I snorted. "That's not it."

She was entirely unconvinced. "Well, your not-date looks quite good in that shirt, don't you think?"

"I hadn't noticed," I said, and refused to look in his direction again. "There. Good as new."

Sorcha beamed and nestled it back on her head. "What would I ever do without you?"

"Have a wedding full of wilted flowers and no floating lanterns," I said, forcing a smile. A familiar tingle was making its way down my nose. "Now shoo, go tell somebody what to do."

For once she listened, and practically skipped off.

Feigning a sneeze, I touched a finger under my nose. Just warm. No blood, thank the gods. Still, I kept my head down and turned back to the arch, finishing the last few blooms with one hand and trembling fingers.

I closed my eyes and reached for my magic, the familiar warmth bloomed in my chest as golden light gathered beneath my skin. A sweet taste filled my mouth, but it was thin and weak like watered-down mead. Drawing from my magic used to feel like dipping a honey comb into a full pot, but lately it felt more like scraping at the crystallized remnants coating the bottom of an empty one.

Glass vessels of every shape lined the table behind me—tavern jars from Brenna's storage, delicate apothecary bottles from Aoife—all waiting for the enchanted flames I'd need to coax inside each of them before dusk. I should've told Sorcha it would have to wait until tomorrow morning and given myself a chance to rest and recover. But I knew how much she wanted to see exactly what everything would look like tomorrow night.

"Ready for this?" said a voice behind me, deep and low and sure.

I didn't have to turn around to know who it was. Goose-bumps prickled up my arms, and that warmth I'd been trying to conjure into my chest finally appeared. I didn't even think it was his voice I was reacting to, so much as the affection I'd unintentionally stitched into the memory of it. My body remembered him before I gave it permission to. I turned anyway, and of course had to look up to meet Calder's eyes—deep green and ringed in gold. Even if the rest of him didn't give him away, those eyes did.

"I'm ready," I said, though the words came out less certain than I'd intended. It felt harder to maintain my composure with him next to me. "There are more lanterns than I remembered."

He glanced at the table laden with glass vessels, then back at me. His gaze swept over the tremor in my hands, the way I was gripping the table's edge. "Good thing there are two of us then."

I closed my eyes and reached for my magic, scraping together what I had left. After enough coaxing, the warm light of it flowed sluggishly through my fingers, and I willed it into the first lantern.

For a moment, the magic in my chest felt warm and strong.

Then, like honey in a cracked jar, it began to drain away again.

"Here," Calder said simply, stepping up beside me. "Why don't I hold them, and you add the fire?"

I let out a slow breath. I had only managed one tiny flame, barely more than kindling, and I wasn't sure I had it in me to try again.

But I didn't have to. Calder handed me the next jar, and with it, a steady flame glowing between his fingers.

He stood close enough that I could smell cedar and woodsmoke clinging to his skin, close enough that what little magic remained in me stirred—traitorous and eager, like it had been waiting for exactly this moment.

"Thank you" I whispered, watching the way his flame danced, perfectly controlled and somehow familiar.

His calloused fingertips brushed mine as I took the flame, and I had to force myself not to wonder what those hands would feel like—the flame in my hands burned brighter than it should have. I focused on transferring the flame to the jar, trying to ignore how much steadier my hands felt than they had moments before.

When I glanced up, Calder's eyes had gone wide, like he was surprised too.

"What?" I asked quietly.

He blinked, as if coming back to himself. "I'm just... the flame took well." He spoke the words slower than usual, and his voice was careful, like he'd had to choose the exact right thing to say.

I turned back to the work, but I could feel him still watching my every move as I reached for the next jar in his hands. Each time he passed me a flame, each time our fingers brushed, my magic grew stronger instead of weaker. The flames burned brighter in my hands, lasted longer, and required less effort to maintain. I refused to acknowledge that I was only slowing down this process, and he could do this without me entirely, his borrowed magic flowing effortlessly into jar after jar. But he didn't give any indication that he would be faster alone. Instead, he seemed content to move in rhythm with me.

By the time we were nearly finished, the meadow glowed around us like we'd captured a constellation, and I felt even better than I had before we started. With all the magic I'd used today, it didn't make sense. I should be exhausted by now.

"There," he said, placing the final flame. "That should do it."

I nodded, flexing my fingers experimentally. They were steady now, no longer trembling. "Thank you. I couldn't have done this alone. Not tonight."

"You could have," he said quietly. "But I'm glad you didn't have to."

Before I could find words to respond, Sorcha's mother appeared, clapping her hands to gather everyone for a rehearsal before the ceremony.

"Meira, you'll walk with Calder," she announced, pairing us together. "Just ahead of Sorcha. Let's make this quick, everyone in position!"

We fell into place, standing behind Brenna and Willem in the procession. Among all the pairs in front of us, the males had offered their partners their arm to hold. When Calder offered me his arm, I hesitated, possibly for a moment too long before taking it. The moment I did place my hand on his forearm though, something crackled through me. The contact hit harder than it should have—like two spells brushing edges, unfinished and waiting. I didn't know if it was magic, or want, or both. Only that it left something humming under my skin.

Something flickered across Calder's face—hurt, maybe, or resignation—before he smoothed his expression into careful neutrality. He adjusted his stance, and took a step to the left, leaving more space between us.

"Sorry," I murmured, hating how raw my voice sounded.

"Don't be," he replied, his own voice low enough that only I could hear. "I get it."

I met his gaze for half a second, then turned away. I didn't want to know if he'd felt that crackling too.

The rehearsal passed in a blur of instructions and positioning, but I was acutely aware of every moment Calder and I moved together. The way he adjusted his pace to match mine. The way his hand covered mine when Sorcha's mother demonstrated how we should stand at the altar. The way he steadied me when I stumbled slightly on the uneven ground.

By the time we finished, it took every bit of my focus to pretend I wasn't completely undone by his proximity.

"Perfect!" Sorcha declared, her eyes bright with excitement. "Now let's go celebrate while there's still wine left in the valley!"

As the group began moving toward Sorcha's family cottage for the rehearsal dinner, Calder fell into step beside me. The evening air had cooled, and I pulled my shawl tighter around my shoulders as we walked the familiar path through the village.

"Thank you," I said quietly, glancing up at him. "For helping with the lanterns. I know Sorcha roped you into more than you bargained for this week."

"She didn't rope me into anything," he said, his voice carrying that same careful tone from earlier. "I offered."

I looked ahead at Sorcha as she walked arm-in-arm with Conor. Calder and I walked in comfortable silence for a moment, our footsteps matching rhythm on the cobblestones. When his arm brushed mine as we navigated around a group of children playing in the street, neither of us moved away.

"Besides," he added quietly, "I think we work well together."

3

———

The sitting room was too small for this many people. The fire crackled and popped in the hearth. The conversations became louder and louder, layered one on top of the other.

Brenna pressed a glass of mulled wine into my hands. Even when she was off work, she couldn't resist playing tavern-keeper. We'd claimed the window seat early, half-hidden by the curtains, watching the celebration unfold around us.

She leaned closer, voice low. "What happened with you and Calder out there?"

I took a long sip instead of answering, letting the warmth of the wine chase away the lingering questions about whatever had passed between us while working on the lanterns. It didn't help as much as I'd hoped.

"Nothing happened," I said finally, but Brenna's knowing look told me I wasn't fooling anyone. She, Sorcha and I had been too close for too long, since we were children stealing apple tarts from the kitchen in this very house. "We just worked well together, I suppose. Though it was strange how easily our magic seemed to..." I trailed off, not sure how to explain what I'd felt.

"Strange how?" Sorcha appeared beside us, her cheeks flushed from wine and joy, clearly having caught the tail end of our conversation.

"Oh, nothing," I said quickly, shooting Brenna a look. "Just that working together was easier than I expected."

"Mm-hmm." Brenna's smile was pure mischief. "Very strange indeed."

"Well, I think it's wonderful," Sorcha said, settling beside us. "You two looked perfect together out there."

"Oh gods, speaking of strange," Brenna leaned in, switching to her tavern-keeper's whisper. "There's been a huge increase in the number of traders coming through the tavern lately. It's not normal for this time of year."

"Where are they going?" Sorcha asked.

"They're all headed to that old castle by the sea, the one the prince from the capitol is restoring. Apparently he's paying double the rate for skilled workers. The tavern's been packed with stone-masons and carpenters, all heading west."

"Double rate?" Conor called from where he stood by the hearth. "For a job by the sea—"

"Don't even think about it," Sorcha cut him off, but she was smiling. "You're not going anywhere." She was joking, but it was true. Nobody ever left Glenmere, at least not for long.

"I've seen it," Calder said quietly from where he now leaned against the doorframe. "It's been a few years though, before the restoration began. But even in ruins, it was beautiful."

I turned toward his voice, caught by the wistfulness in it. Through the window, the last rays of sunlight caught the peaks of the western mountains. It had been awhile since I'd thought about it last, but now I couldn't help and wonder what was beyond them. I imagined somewhere beyond them, about the people bringing that ancient castle back to life. I'd only ever seen castles in books, sketches of towers and battlements.

"What was it like?" I found myself asking before I could stop myself.

Calder's gaze found mine across the room. "I could never do it justice," he said, shaking his head. "It sits on its own cliff, and you could only get to it by walking a long bridge. The stone towers looked like they'd risen straight out of the land beneath them. If I think about it, I can still hear the waves crashing below. Even though it was crumbling when I saw it, you could see how magnificent it must have been."

"More wine?" Sorcha asked, already reaching for my cup, but I barely heard her. I was too busy imagining what it would be like to stand on those cliffs, to see the ocean stretching endlessly beyond.

Before I could ask more, Sorcha's mother swept into the room, flour-dusted apron and all, a huge grin on her face. "To the dining room, everyone! Before it all gets cold. Sorcha, honey, can you show everyone their seats?"

I found myself directed to a seat beside Calder, close enough that our elbows touched, making it impossible to focus on the platters being passed or the conversation flowing around us.

"Could you pass the bread?" Calder's low voice brought me back to the moment.

Our fingers brushed as I handed it over, and I felt that same crackling warmth from the meadow.

Across the table, Conor was regaling everyone with the story of how he'd first met Sorcha, flinging his hands wildly as he described being unable to take his eyes off of her, and subsequently falling into the creek.

Sorcha's mother kept passing dishes, insisting everyone take seconds, thirds. Someone mentioned the weather for tomorrow's ceremony, and a debate sparked up about the best preservation charms for outdoor celebrations.

I should have joined that conversation, but all I could focus on was the movement of Calder's hands, the way his fingers moved and flexed as he carefully buttered his bread. Every twist of his wrist sent his magic brushing against mine, like fingers dragging down my spine from the inside.

"—don't you think, Meira?"

Brenna was looking right at me, her eyes glittering with amusement. She had asked me something, and from her knowing smile, probably more than once.

"About the preservation charms," she prompted. "For the ceremony tomorrow. You'd know best, being our resident expert and all."

"Right," I said, grateful for familiar ground. "The key is layering different types of preservation magic depending on what you're protecting. For cut flowers, you want to seal the stems first to prevent wilting, then add a color-lock charm so they don't fade. But for living arrangements like the arch, you need something gentler—more of a sustaining spell that works with the plant's natural magic rather than overriding it."

"See? Told you she'd know," Brenna said to the rest of the table.

Calder shifted beside me, and his knee brushed against mine under the table. Steam curled up from my untouched soup, and I focused on watching it rise instead of the warmth coiling low in my belly.

But it was no use, the heat from his touch rushed through me, my blood molten in my veins. I needed air. I needed space.

I stood too quickly as I tried to make my escape, and the room tilted. Firelight swelled and narrowed in my vision, the voices in the room distorting like echoes in a well.

My knees buckled.

My hip knocked the edge of the table, rattling the silverware and sending someone's spoon to the floor. The conversations faltered, and several heads turned.

A firm hand caught my elbow before I could fall.

"Careful," Calder murmured. He'd turned in his seat and was offering me his other hand.

"Just got up too fast," I said, taking his outstretched hand to steady myself. The room was still spinning slightly, and I realized how foolish I must look, making a dramatic exit only to nearly faint in the process. "Too much wine, maybe."

He didn't release my hand until I sat back down, his thumb brushing once across my knuckles before he let go.

"Are you alright, dear?" Sorcha's mother asked in a hushed tone, her brow creased when she noticed my untouched soup. The wooden spoon tucked into her apron pocket knocked softly against her chair as she leaned forward. "You look a bit peaked."

"I'm fine," I assured her, attempting a smile. The wine had left a warm, spiced taste on my tongue. "Just tired. It's been a long day of preparations."

She reached across the table to squeeze my hand. It was such a simple, motherly gesture, but I did not want her to stop. I wanted her to hold my hand, to give me something to lean into, just long enough to remember what it felt like when my own mother had been around. "We're so grateful for everything you've done, Meira. Sorcha's lucky to have a friend like you."

The warmth in her voice made my throat tight. "She'd do the same for me."

As the evening wound down, I helped clear dishes, moving easily around the familiar kitchen while the others continued their conversations in the dining room. When everything was cleared, I gathered my things so I could walk home, but my bag wasn't where I remembered leaving it.

I scanned the sitting room again, then slipped down the hallway toward the front door. Maybe Brenna or Sorcha had hung it on the coatrack. But when I turned the corner, Calder was there.

He stood near the front door, one hand wrapped around the worn leather strap of my bag, like he'd been holding it for a while. He didn't offer it to me.

"I'll walk you home," he said.

"That's very kind, but I can manage on my own." I reached for my bag, but he didn't let go.

"You nearly hit the floor earlier," he said gently.

I rolled my eyes, heat already creeping up my neck. "It was just the wine, like I said. I'm perfectly fine now."

"I know you are," he said. "But it's late. It's dark. And—"

"Calder." I met his eyes directly. "I appreciate the offer, truly. But I've been walking these streets my entire life. I know every stone, every turn. I'll be fine."

He studied my face for a long moment, and I could see him weighing his words. Finally, his grip on my bag loosened. "If you're sure."

"I am." I took the bag from him, managing a small smile. "Thank you, though. For offering. And for tonight."

"Of course." He stepped back, giving me space to reach the door. "Goodnight, Meira."

"Goodnight," I said, and meant it.

I walked out into the cool night air, feeling his eyes on me until I was several yards down the path and finally heard the door creak shut behind me.

I almost made it to the corner before I stopped.

The stars were bright. The road ahead was familiar. And still, I didn't want to walk it alone.

Not tonight.

Not after the way his magic had warmed my fingers. Not after the way he'd looked at me during dinner like he couldn't quite stop. Not after every quiet thing he hadn't said.

So I turned back, and only had to knock on the door once, because it opened almost immediately.

Calder stood on the other side, still holding himself like he hadn't moved, like he'd been hoping I'd come back.

"I changed my mind," I said, lifting my chin. "Walk me home."

His expression didn't shift much, but something eased. He let out the faintest exhale, and there was a softening at the corner of his mouth.

"Alright."

We didn't speak as we walked.

Not because there was nothing to say, but because the silence between us felt full and intentional. Comfort blooming slowly in the dark.

Our hands never touched, but they stayed inches apart the whole way home.

Even though we didn't make contact, I felt every near-miss. His fingers brushed the air beside mine as we walked. The deliberate way he matched my pace, like we'd done this a hundred times before. I'd never let myself think of him like this. Now I couldn't think of anything else.

feast, and even laughing at old Hamish's stories as he recounted various village weddings from throughout the years. For the first time in as long as I could remember, I wasn't worried about anything that needed to be done tomorrow.

"Meira!" Sorcha appeared at my elbow, practically glowing with happiness. "Have you danced yet?"

Her copper hair glowed in the golden light of sunset, which made the tiny enchantments I'd woven into her flower crown shimmer like captured fireflies. Over the last few weeks, I'd poured what felt like half my soul into this wedding, but seeing her so happy made it worth every drop of magic.

"I've been mingling," I said, which was true. "Congratulating people, sampling your mother's excellent cake…"

"That's not dancing," she said, before squeezing my hand. "Are you feeling okay? Your eyes look a bit…" she trailed off. The genuine concern in her voice made my throat tighten.

"I'm a little tired, but who cares about me?" I teased, and gave her a wide smile. "The only thoughts in that pretty head of yours should be about how much wine you can drink tonight without falling asleep before you consummate your marriage."

She laughed, but didn't give up. "And yours should be out there dancing!" She leaned in and spoke quieter, so that only I could hear her. "I have it on good authority that a certain someone has been hoping you'd say yes if he asked."

Before I could ask what she meant, I felt a presence behind me.

"Excuse me," said a familiar voice. "I was wondering if I might steal the bride's friend for a dance?"

I turned to find Calder, looking slightly nervous. He'd rolled up his sleeves, and the hope in his eyes paired with the casual confidence in his stance made my heart skip.

"I was just telling her she needs to dance," Sorcha said with a guilty smile on her face. "Weren't I, Meira?"

I looked between them, suddenly understanding that this had been planned. "Have the two of you been conspiring?"

"Absolutely," Calder said without shame. "Is it working?"

I couldn't help but laugh. "One dance," I said, taking his offered hand. "But I'm warning you, I might step on your feet."

"I'll risk it," he said, and led me toward the other couples.

The music was slower now, a traditional valley song played at most celebrations that I'd recognized since childhood. Calder's hand was warm and steady at my waist, his other hand clasped around mine as he guided me through the steps. Each time he guided me through a turn, his hand eased from my waist onto my back, and he pressed slightly firmer, like he didn't want to let me drift too far away.

"You're not stepping on my feet," he observed after we'd been dancing for a few moments.

"The song is still young, there's still time," I replied, and he chuckled.

One song turned into a few, and what felt like hours of dancing, Sorcha's mother pulled Calder away, needing his help to replace the empty barrel of mead.

I sagged in relief against the refreshment table, grateful for the moment alone to collect myself. The familiar iron taste lingered on my tongue, and I reached for a cup of wine to wash it away. All the spinning and twirling had left me dizzy, and the effects of the morning's magic work were catching up with me.

"You look like you could use a partner."

I recognized Nolan's voice immediately, smooth as molasses and twice as sticky. Of course he would choose this moment to appear, when I was one wrong move away from ending up face-first in the punch bowl.

"I wondered where my favorite Wardcrafter was hiding," he said, his smile bright enough to draw answering grins from nearby guests.

I hated being referred to by only my title.

"Lovely ceremony, wasn't it? Though I have to say..." He nodded toward where Sorcha and Conor swayed together, lost in their own world. "There's nothing quite like watching two people who belong together."

He wasn't wrong about the newlyweds, they did look perfect together. But the way he was looking at my mouth as he said it made my skin crawl. That predatory grin that followed, like the two of us were sharing a private joke, made my stomach turn.

"That could be us next," his voice dropped as he said it, which made it sound almost intimate. "We were good together once. You and I, we could be here doing that exact thing." He stepped closer. "Especially now that you've had time to... move on."

The audacity took my breath away. *Move on?*

As if I could forget how he'd shown up at my door the day after my parents' funeral. We'd been seeing each other casually when they passed, but he wasted no time trying to convince me how much sense it made for us to marry quickly, about combining our households and what he was planning for my shop to make it more profitable.

Before my mother and father were even in the ground, he'd been making plans. I'd ended things as soon as I realized he saw my grief as an opportunity.

"What could be us? Dancing?" I asked innocently, pretending I'd misunderstood, buying time until I found a way out of the conversation. "I'm a bit tired from all the celebrating."

"No, Meira," he said, shaking his head with that condescending smile I remembered too well. "You know the elders have been discussing your future. With how tired you've looked lately, it's clear you need someone to help carry the burden your parents left for you."

The words landed like cold hands around my throat. Did he really think I'd become more pliable? That I'd forgotten how quickly he'd tried to take over my life when I was at my weakest?

"But speaking of dancing..." He offered his hand. "Shall we?"

"Meira's with me for the evening," a voice cut in—low, calm, and edged with steel.

Calder.

He appeared beside me as if he'd known I needed help.

"Sorry to interrupt," he said, his hard gaze was fixed on Nolan, but his voice remained smooth, "but she already agreed to spend the evening with me." He offered me his hand before continuing, "And I've never been good at sharing."

I hadn't realized how tight I was clenching my jaw until the tension eased at the sight of him. He looked at me with a quiet question in his eyes, like he was asking, *Are you okay?*

I am now, I thought.

Nolan's expression didn't just fall, it hardened into stone. His eyes flicked between Calder and me, and I could tell this wasn't over. Even though Calder had lived in the village for two years and was loved by most, there were still valley fae like Nolan who kept their distance from outsiders.

For a moment, I thought he might actually challenge Calder right here in front of everyone. But then forced a practiced smile back onto his face. "Another time, then," he said smoothly, but the tone of his voice felt more like a threat.

Calder's hand settled confidently at my waist, and my breath caught. The touch was possessive in a way that made my skin burn beneath the fabric of my dress. I wanted to lean into his solid warmth, to let him shield me from more than just Nolan's unwanted attention, but it felt selfish to put that on him. His thumb pressed just slightly against my ribs, and I wondered if he could feel my heart hammering against my chest.

He adjusted our stance so that he could offer me more

support, but to anyone watching, we looked like any other couple. Only Calder would know he was holding me up.

Beyond the dancing couples and the lantern light, the mountains rose dark against the stars. Somewhere up there, I bet Calder had walked paths I'd never see. He'd seen countless villages I'd never visit. The wards needed daily attention and even a short trip would leave the village vulnerable. Just like my mother, I'd spend my life watching those peaks from below.

"Thank you," I managed. "For stepping in. You didn't have to do that."

"I'd take any chance to see Nolan's face turn that particular shade of purple." The corner of Calder's mouth quirked up. "I knew it would be worth whatever price I'll eventually have to pay."

"You two have history?" I asked, trying not to sound as interested as I was.

"Let's just say he's never been comfortable with someone like me settling here. And he really doesn't like fae who don't show the proper deference to his family name." His voice dropped, eyes flickering toward where Nolan had disappeared into the crowd. "Though I suspect I've just given him a much better reason to despise me."

I couldn't stop the satisfied smile from spreading across my face.

We moved together naturally, and for a few blissful moments, I let myself get lost in the rhythm. The music was sweet, Calder's arms were strong, and I could almost forget about everything I had been feeling.

But the familiar iron taste was creeping back onto my tongue.

I stumbled, and Calder's grip tightened instantly, steadying me.

"Maybe we should sit down," he murmured. "I see two spots

right over there. I'll walk you over and then get us something to eat."

"I'm fine," I said automatically, even as the edges of my vision started to blur. "I just need a moment."

"Meira." His voice was gentle but firm. "You're not fine."

I wanted to argue, but another wave of dizziness hit me. All the magic I'd poured into the morning preparations, the dancing, the wine on an empty stomach, the anger I'd felt at Nolan —it was all catching up to me at once.

I couldn't fall. Not here, not now. Not after two years of proving I was stronger than that. Not with Calder watching. Not again.

"Let's rest for a bit," Calder said, already guiding me toward the edge of the celebration.

But my legs stopped moving, and the lanterns above us began to blur and blend together. The sounds of the party grew distant, voices echoing as if from underwater.

"Calder," I whispered, my fingers tightening on his shirt.

"I've got you," he promised, but his voice sounded far away.

The world tilted hard, and darkness crept in from the edges of my vision.

I felt myself falling, but I didn't hit the ground. Calder didn't let me.

The last thing I remembered was being lifted into his arms, the steady beat of his heart against my cheek. Just like two years ago. But this time I wasn't alone, and instead of shame, I felt safe.

5

———

I woke to the smell of tea and an ache that felt like it had started in my bones and settled everywhere else. Every point of contact with the mattress hurt—hips, shoulders, elbows, even the backs of my heels. My back felt like it had been packed with stones, and every breath shifted them deeper. My joints throbbed and whatever was left of my magic had curled tight behind my ribs, and made it hard to breathe.

The window was cracked open, just enough to let in the cool morning air. Sunlight spilled across the floorboards in a narrow band I'd seen a hundred times before.

Home.

Relief came in a calming rush, followed immediately by the memories of the rest of the night. The wedding. The dancing. The reception. The dizziness. The part where I collapsed in front of half the valley.

The part where Calder caught me.

"Meira?"

Brenna's voice was close, quiet in the way people speak around sleeping babies.

I turned toward her, and pain lanced through my skull like

someone had driven an iron spike behind my eyes. I hissed through my teeth, and clutched at the blanket. Brenna reached for me instantly.

"She's awake!" she called out to whoever else was here, and then she was kneeling at my bedside. She brushed the hair off of my forehead.

Aoife hurried in, looking like she'd slept in a chair. Her gray braid was unraveling, and the usual feistiness in her eyes had been dulled by fatigue.

"Easy," Brenna murmured, pressing a cool palm to my forehead. "You've been out most of the day."

My throat felt like sandpaper. "The wedding..."

"Was beautiful and the night was almost over anyways," Brenna said firmly. "Though you did give everyone still there quite the scare."

I closed my eyes. Of course I had.

"Sorcha wanted to take you home with her," Brenna added, and snorted with a soft laugh before she could stop herself. "She said she didn't care if it was her wedding night. She wanted you set up in the guest room, and she promised to sleep right next to your bed. You should have seen Conor's face."

"I told her that was unnecessary," Aoife said, pulling a tin from her bag. "You were stable, just exhausted. But she only agreed to go home because Calder promised to stay and watch over you."

"He did," Brenna added when I didn't respond. "He carried you here himself and refused to leave. He's been pacing the kitchen all night."

"Is he still here?" I asked, surprised by how much I wanted to know.

"Aoife finally kicked him out a bit ago." Brenna said.

"I sent him out for fresh air and food," Aoife said. "He was wearing a hole in the floor."

As if he knew we'd been talking about him, I heard the

front door open and careful footsteps in the hallway. Then Calder appeared in the doorway still wearing yesterday's clothes.

His shirt was wrinkled and hanging open at the collar, sleeves pushed up to reveal those forearms that had been haunting my thoughts. Dark stubble shadowed his jaw, and his hair looked like he'd run his hands through it a dozen times. He looked exhausted, worried, and somehow more appealing than anyone had a right to look after staying up all night.

"You're awake," he said, and I thought it sounded like relief in his voice.

I nodded, suddenly self-conscious about how I must look.

"How are you feeling?" he asked, and stepped into the room.

"Like a horse stepped on my head," I admitted.

That earned me a small smile.

"Thank you," I said quietly. "For catching me. For staying. You didn't have to do that."

"You don't need to thank me for that," he replied, and his tone made my chest warm despite how much the rest of my body hurt.

There was a knock at the front door, then two more in quick succession. Whoever was on the other side didn't have much patience.

"It's the elders. They've been trying to get in here since dawn." Calder clenched his jaw. "I'll go talk to them," he said as he stood to leave.

"Let them come," I said, though my voice shook. "I'll have to face them sometime." I tried to sit up straighter, but Aoife pushed me back down with a firm hand.

"You're not getting out of that bed. Let them come to you for once," she said, and she went to the door to let them in.

Low voices filtered in and then the sound of Elder Thomas's boots on my floorboards, his steps were heavy and entitled, like he wanted everyone to know when he arrived.

Elder Muriel opened the door slowly and peaked her head around first before entering quietly, doing her best not to disturb me. Elder Thomas followed, he had no such concerns. Worst of all, Nolan shuffled in on his tail.

"Meira, dear," Elder Muriel said as she entered, voice warm with concern. "We came as soon as we heard."

"I'm fine," I said on instinct. "Just overextended my magic a bit with all of the wedding preparations."

Elder Thomas cleared his throat, the frown he always wore plastered on his face. "This goes beyond 'overdoing it,' Meira. You collapsed in front of half the village. There are children asking if you're dying."

"If she was, it's because she's been burning herself out to keep them safe," Brenna said from behind them, her arms folded.

Thomas didn't acknowledge her.

I fought the urge to roll my eyes. "I'm not dying."

"No," Aoife agreed, measuring dried herbs into small pouches with practiced movements. "Not this time, but I don't see any sense in trying to make it so."

"Which is why we're here," Muriel said. "The Council has been... concerned about your situation for some time now."

"My situation is fine," I said, even as the room swam at the edges of my vision. "I've managed just fine for two years."

"This is exactly why the wardcraft requires two people," Thomas said bluntly. "You can't keep draining yourself like this and expect to remain upright. When you go down, the village is left vulnerable."

"Your parents worked together for good reason," Elder Muriel added, her voice gentler but no less firm. "You've carried too much for too long, and no one's doubting your strength. But this—" she gestured toward Meira's pale, still form, "—this is not what your parents would have wanted for you."

I wanted to argue, but what could I say? That I was fine and could keep going? There wasn't much I could say in my own defense as I lay in bed under the covers.

"And now we have no one monitoring the wards at all," Thomas continued, his agitation growing. "Do you know what happened the last time we had an extended gap in ward maintenance? Garden gnomes destroyed half the vegetable plots. Water sprites drove all of the fish out of the valley's stretch of river and it was weeks before we saw another one. And that was only a couple of days without proper coverage."

"So what are you suggesting?" I asked, though I already knew I wouldn't like the answer.

And then Nolan stepped forward. "The Council has discussed potential partnerships," he said, his voice measured and reasonable. "I've expressed my willingness to take on that responsibility. We have history, Meira. We understand each other."

He said it so easily, like it hadn't taken everything in me to keep this valley standing, like he hadn't watched me drain myself for years and still thought I should be grateful to be chosen. Grateful for his offer to let me keep working—as if I needed permission, as if my mother's tools and my father's magic were things I might hand over like a dowry. And he'd felt comfortable enough in present company to say it. As if this was reasonable, a kindness.

Brenna made a sound of pure disbelief.

Nolan continued as if she wasn't even there.

"This isn't a criticism," Nolan said, folding his hands. "You've done more than anyone expected. But it's clearly too much. You need help, Meira. And not just anyone, but someone like me who understands what this job takes. Someone who already knows how you work. We could have what your parents had. Better, even."

My fingers curled into the blanket, forming into a fist tight enough that my knuckles ached. I could smell the faint hint of blood, but didn't feel it yet. My magic flared in protest, even though it was weak. The casual way he discussed my life, my work, my parents felt as if everything I was and everything I'd built were just pieces on a board to be reorganized for efficiency.

"That's enough."

The voice came from the corner of the room, and every head turned. Thomas actually startled, his eyes widening as he saw Calder.

He'd been there the whole time, but Muriel, Thomas, and Nolan looked surprised, as if they were noticing him for the first time.

Calder didn't raise his voice but he didn't need to. His voice was a command that moved through the room with weight, sharp enough to make everyone go still.

He crossed the room slowly and positioned himself between me and the Council before settling in the chair beside my bed.

For a moment, no one said anything. I wasn't sure anyone could.

My mother once told me that the forest fae never severed their ties to the ancient magic. That they were still bound to old rules in ways most of us had long since forgotten—rules that offered power, yes, but demanded obedience in return.

She said they couldn't speak untruths. That if they tried, their own magic would turn on them. I used to think that must have limited them. That it must have made them predictable, even, harmless.

Most valley fae liked to pretend forest fae were lesser. Simpler. Like our distance from the wild made us superior to it.

Looking at Calder Byrne now—calm, unmoved, undeniable —I realized I had no idea what he was truly capable of.

Muriel blinked, looking faintly disoriented. Even Nolan

seemed unsettled, his arrogant posture wavering as he took in Calder's presence.

"If security is the concern," Calder said, his voice calm but firm, "I can stand guard while Meira recovers."

Elder Thomas scoffed. "You? One outsider patrolling our entire valley perimeter?"

"If you want more people, then I'll organize a proper guard rotation," Calder replied without missing a beat. "Recruit volunteers from the village. Males like Conor, Willem—people who know the land and care about protecting it."

Muriel perked up. "That could work. A patrol while Meira recovers."

Thomas grumbled, but he wouldn't openly argue with another elder outside of the Council chamber. "Temporary," he said finally. "And unofficial. Just until she's well enough to resume her duties."

"Of course," Calder agreed. "But someone needs to watch the perimeter. I can coordinate that."

"You'd do that?" I asked, surprised by the offer.

"The valley needs protection," he said simply. "You need rest. It makes sense."

Thomas was still frowning, but Muriel nodded approvingly. "See that you establish patrols by tomorrow. Report any irregularities to the Council immediately."

"And in the meantime," Thomas added, his tone grudging, "we'll discuss longer-term solutions for the wardcraft itself."

After they left, Brenna let out a low whistle. "Well, that was something."

"That was brave," I said to Calder, though my voice came out flatter than I intended. "Or stupid. I haven't decided."

He laughed, "I guess it depends on whatever tries to get through while you're gone."

"Thank you," I added. "I mean it."

He shrugged. "Someone has to watch the valley while you recover. Might as well be people who actually care about it."

"I can help," Brenna offered. "Connect you with the right people. Half the village drinks at my tavern, so I know who's reliable."

"That would be useful," Calder said, looking grateful for the offer.

"Most people wouldn't have thought to step up like that," I said quietly.

"Most people don't..." He stopped himself, he seemed to think better of whatever he'd been about to say. "It's what needs to be done."

"They're going to replace me," I said. I hadn't meant to say it out loud.

"That's not what they're saying." Calder said softly, then shook his head like he couldn't quite believe it either.

I turned my head just enough to see him lower himself back into the chair closest to the bed. He didn't meet my eyes right away.

"If they wanted you gone, they'd have done it after the first collapse," he said. "This... this feels more like marriage."

The word marriage landed between my ribs like a dagger. I didn't argue—he already knew how far back this went, and he wasn't wrong. But knowing it didn't make it any easier to swallow.

Aoife returned, looking satisfied. "That's quite enough excitement for me for one morning. Meira, I've laid some sachets of herbs downstairs, I want you to take them for tea twice daily. No wardwork or magic whatsoever for at least a week."

"A week?" I protested. "The wards can't go untended that long."

"They won't be," Calder said. "The guard will keep watch."

"And I'll make sure people actually show up for their shifts,"

Brenna added with a grin. "It's amazing how motivated people get when their favorite barmaid asks for a favor."

"One week," Aoife said firmly. "I have to leave now, I have a few other patients to see today, but I'll check back with you in a couple of days."

She paused at the door. "And Meira? Try to find something restful to do with your hands while you recover."

After Aoife left, Brenna stood and stretched. "I should head back to the tavern, start recruiting." She squeezed my shoulder. "Get some rest."

After she left too, the room fell quiet. Calder remained in his chair, staring out the window. He looked exhausted.

"Thank you," I said finally. "For stepping in like that."

He rubbed his face with both hands. "I should probably go find Conor, get this patrol thing sorted." He stood, then paused at the door. "Try to actually rest, alright? No sneaking out to check on anything."

"I wouldn't—"

"You would." The corner of his mouth quirked up. "Sleep, Meira."

"Have you done this before?"

He paused at the door with a smirk tugging at the corner of his mouth. "I wasn't always a woodworker, Meira."

Then he crossed back to my bedside, took my hand, and pressed a quick kiss to the back of it.

And then he was gone.

I stared at the empty doorway, the ghost of his kiss still warm on my skin, and wondered what was happening between us—and what, if anything, I was supposed to do about it—right up until the moment I fell asleep.

6

———

The first day of forced rest almost felt like a gift.

I slept until late morning, waking to the smell of fresh bread, and went to the kitchen to find Brenna had left a still-warm loaf on the table. I ate it standing, barefoot and still in my nightgown, savoring the freedom of having nowhere to be.

Aoife stopped by mid-morning, looking me over like I was a prize goat at the market. "Try to enjoy this, Meira," she said, patting my hand with gentle concern. She left me with more bitter tea and strict orders not to light so much as a candle.

Day two, the peace started to itch.

I woke at dawn out of habit, but instead of getting out of bed, I grabbed one of the books from my nightstand that I'd been meaning to read for years. I read three chapters before I couldn't stand to be still anymore.

Brenna brought vegetable soup around noon, and stayed to 'keep me company,' but I suspected she was supervising to make sure I ate.

"Ran into Calder on my way over," she mentioned, swirling

her spoon around her bowl. "He'd been out at the northern boundary this morning, walking the woods."

"Did he say anything else?" I tried to sound casual. My own spoon hovered, forgotten, halfway to my mouth, while my heartbeat picked up like it always did when someone said his name.

"Not really," she said, shrugging. "You know how he is though."

I didn't really, but I also didn't know how to ask what she meant without revealing how desperately I wanted to know everything about him.

After she left, I found myself pacing in front of the window, stopping every so often to look toward the street. Just in case he walked by, I might be able to catch a glimpse of him.

I hadn't heard anything about the wards, so they must be holding so far. That, or Calder and his small army were handling things just fine. The thought of him out there, checking the boundaries, taking care of what I couldn't—it should have made me feel grateful.

Instead, it made me ache.

Day three, I woke up restless.

Restless because I was lying here useless while he was out there protecting the village. Restless because a part of me that I was trying to ignore, was grateful someone else was carrying the weight. Restless because I couldn't stop thinking about the way he'd caught me, carried me, stayed with me.

I was even restless because every time I closed my eyes, I could still feel the steady rhythm of his heartbeat against my cheek.

On the fourth morning, I walked the full perimeter and didn't find a single weakness. I knew I couldn't do anything about it, even if I found one, but I walked stone to stone anyways. Followed the perimeter, slow and methodical in my scrutiny, and didn't find a single weak spot.

Maybe I'd misread the patterns, misjudged the hum of the magic beneath my palms. But everywhere I looked the wards were threaded with strength and humming in such a steady rhythm, they were almost impossible to hear.

I crossed the wooden bridge over the river toward the eastern stone and paused, letting myself linger just a little longer than necessary. The water was clear this morning, so still that I watched a few bright fish swim lazily around smooth stones as easily as if I'd been looking through glass.

The eastern wardstone pulsed with quiet, effortless power.

I should have felt relieved that everything had been taken care of in my absence. I should have let that ease settle over me, should have let myself relax into it for once. But knowing that the one thing I'd rebuilt my life around, holding the wards together with my own two hands, didn't even need me anymore left me feeling hollow.

I stayed at the eastern stone until the sun crept high enough to fully crest the mountain before eventually turning towards town. I had to be cleared by Aoife, but I hoped I could return to my shop today. Her cottage sat on the northern edge of town. If I went straight to town from here, I'd have to walk past the square, past the morning crowd at the bakery, and past all of the people who would either gawk or ask several, likely personal, questions.

So I took the long way around to Aoife's, walking down the path lined with moss-covered stones, admiring the flower boxes beneath her windowsills and the lemony scent of trailing verbena. The gate creaked under my hand, and when I got closer, I heard voices.

I slowed my steps. The window was open. One of the voices was Aoife, and the other—

My heart stumbled. Calder.

I didn't mean to stop walking. But I found myself hovering

beside Aoife's flower box with my arms crossed tight over my ribs, trying to make myself small and still.

I knew better than to eavesdrop, but I couldn't make myself move.

"Tell me what's bothering you," Aoife said, her voice smooth as ever. I heard the clink of glass as she moved around inside.

"I'm not sleeping much." Calder's voice was more quiet and shy than I'd ever heard.

Aoife didn't comment on it right away. Just the faint rustle of her skirts, the creak of wood beneath weight—Calder settling onto the treatment table. I would recognize that sound anywhere. I'd laid on that table more times than I cared to count.

"Is that why you've been out at the wards before daylight?"

"Partially." A pause. "I'd go regardless, though."

"I know you would," she said.

Aoife hummed, low and wordless, which meant she was looking him over. I'd never asked if it was part of her magic, or if it was just something she did to keep her hands steady while she worked.

A long silence stretched out, quiet enough that I almost turned to leave—until she spoke again.

"Well," she said, "the good news is there's nothing seriously wrong. You're just feeling the effects of stress."

"Stress?" Calder asked, incredulous. "What am I stressed about?"

I wondered that too. He always seemed so calm, like nothing in the world had enough weight to drag him under.

"Caring about people does that to us," Aoife said, and her voice was different this time.

Another shift of weight on the table. Calder sat up.

"Have you been checking on her often?" Aoife asked.

"I haven't seen her," Calder said, and it made my chest tighten. "I didn't want to intrude."

"Mm," Aoife hummed, the cadence all-knowing. "Maybe that's the stress."

A deep exhale from Calder, and he let out a sound that was almost a laugh and almost a groan. "She works too hard."

"I know."

"She can't keep going like this."

"I agree."

"I don't know how to help her," he said, his voice lower now. "I don't think she'd let me."

My heart hammered against my ribs. He wanted to help me. He was losing sleep over me.

"You're probably right," Aoife said. "Though right now, she doesn't have much choice."

They fell silent again. For one heartbeat, two.

Then Calder's voice, barely audible, said, "Back at her house in front of the Council elders—you said something that made it sound like you didn't think she was too far from burning herself out completely."

He didn't ask the question.

But Aoife answered it anyway. "I meant it."

I pressed my hand to my mouth, fighting the urge to make a sound.

"I've seen it happen before," Calder continued, voice rough. "When someone gives everything, burns through their magic, that kind of burning... it doesn't just take the magic. It takes everything."

I stared down at the ground, my vision blurred behind a tear forming in each of my eyes. Was I so pathetic and starved for affection that just hearing someone might care if I died was enough to make me cry?

Apparently, yes.

My boots were scuffed. My right one was untied. A rock sat half-buried at the edge of the walkway, and I nudged it with the toe of my shoe, desperate for something, anything, to focus on besides the ache spreading through my chest.

I stepped back from the window, pulse too loud in my ears. I couldn't face them. Not like this.

I turned and walked quickly down the path, letting the stones guide my steps without looking back. The gate creaked shut behind me, and I kept going.

By the time I reached my cottage, my fingers fumbled the latch, too clumsy to cooperate. Inside, the silence hit me all at once. Too still. Too sharp. The walls felt smaller than I remembered.

I sank into the chair by the window and stared at the empty street.

When my parents died, people checked on me because that's what you do when someone loses everything. When I collapsed at the wedding, they worried because no wardcrafter meant a vulnerable village. Even Sorcha's fierce loyalty felt like an extension of our childhood bond—something built from years of shared secrets and sleepovers.

But Calder wasn't acting out of obligation. He'd shown up that first day as a stranger with no ties to this place, no reason to care what happened to the girl he found in the grass. He could have walked away a dozen times since. Should have, probably.

Instead, he'd organized guard patrols and lost sleep worrying about me. He just seemed to care. And I hadn't even done anything for him to earn it.

THE NEXT AFTERNOON, I was halfway through the same book I'd been trying to read for days, when someone knocked at my door. It was too heavy-handed to be Brenna or Aoife.

When I opened the door, Calder stood on my threshold with his hands shoved in his pockets. "Hi."

"Hi," I bit back a smile and stepped aside to let him in.

He hesitated for a moment before stepping inside. "Aoife said you were supposed to see her yesterday. It didn't seem like you to not show up, so I thought I'd check on you."

"I didn't feel up for the walk."

"Right." He glanced around the cottage, taking in the scattered books and cold hearth. "How are you feeling? Really?"

"Better. Restless, mostly," I said, and it wasn't entirely a lie.

If I was completely honest, I would have said, *I'm much more used to working myself into the ground day in and day out so now that I have some actual time for myself, I don't know what to do and I think I'm losing my mind.*

But instead I said, "I'm not used to sitting still for so long."

"I can imagine." His expression warmed slightly. "Though you might be interested to know that your enforced rest has led to some interesting developments with the patrol."

"Oh?"

"Yesterday Willem decided he could track better if he climbed a tree. But it turns out he's not actually very good at it. He got up there just fine, but then he spent two hours stuck fifteen feet up an oak before Conor could talk him down." His eyes crinkled with suppressed laughter.

"And the Murphy boys thought they could cover more ground if they split up, but we found each of them asleep against a different wardstone a few hours later."

I couldn't help but laugh. "Please tell me no one has been injured while the guards have been doing everything except guarding."

"Miraculously, no. Though Hamish did insist on bringing his prized hunting hound, who immediately ran off chasing his own tail and had to be retrieved from Mrs. Blackwood's herb garden."

"Poor Mrs. Blackwood."

"She was surprisingly understanding. I think she's just

happy to have an excuse to fuss over the 'brave young men protecting our valley.'" He mimicked her voice perfectly, and I cackled embarrassingly loud.

As humiliating as it was, it felt good to laugh. I'd forgotten how easy Calder was to be around when I wasn't overthinking every word.

"Sit," I said, gesturing toward the small couch. "Please. You're making me nervous hovering in my doorway like that."

He settled onto the couch, and I curled up in the chair across from him, tucking my feet under me.

"The good news is that despite everything, the boundaries are secure. No signs of anything more dangerous than overly curious woodland creatures."

"That's a relief." The last time a ward section had weakened enough to let something through, it was my first summer working them alone. We'd lost half the village gardens to hungry gnomes, three beehives to sugar-mad pixies, and an entire cherry harvest to the orchard imps.

The villagers had only just stopped grumbling about the summer we went without pie.

"How did you get a patrol together so quickly? Do you have experience raising small armies?" I asked it like a joke, though I was genuinely curious about his past.

Something shifted in his expression, became more careful. "I've had to organize groups before. Make sure people knew what they were supposed to be doing and when."

"What kind of groups?"

He was quiet for a moment, like he was choosing his words. "Security details, mostly. Making sure people got where they needed to go safely."

That was the kind of answer someone gave when they wouldn't be sharing any more details.

"But it also meant I got to see places most people never do," He offered. "Moors that stretch for miles without a single tree, just purple heather and wind. Lochs that reflect the mountains so perfectly you can't tell where the water ends and the sky begins."

"What else?" I wanted to hear about everything he'd seen.

"There's a valley about three days north of here where hot springs bubble up through colored stone. The water's warm enough to swim in even when snow covers the ground."

"I've never seen a hot spring. I haven't seen much beyond the valley, really."

He met my eyes. "I'll take you, if you want. When you're feeling stronger, until Aoife clears you for longer trips, maybe I could show you some of the closer places. Nothing too far from the wards, but there are places even within a day's ride that most valley folk have never seen."

"You'd want to do that?"

"If you're interested, then yes. I'd like that."

"I am," I said, a little too quickly. It wasn't the kind of offer I was used to getting. "I've always wanted to travel but I've never had the chance."

"Well, now you will. When you're ready."

The promise in those words settled into my chest. It was the first thing I'd looked forward to in longer than I could remember.

"Tell me more," I said. "About the places you've seen."

He told me about stone bridges built by people whose names had been forgotten, about markets in coastal towns where you could buy things from lands across the sea. I asked him what the people were like, what they ate, how they spoke. The questions kept coming, and he answered each one like he was pleased I wanted to know.

When the conversation died down, I realized we'd been unconsciously leaning toward each other. He sat on the very edge of the couch now, his hands clasped between his knees, while I'd curled forward in my chair until we were close enough that I could see the gold flecks in his eyes clearly.

"You realize you're being cruel, don't you?" I said, settling back in my chair with a small smile. "Making me want things I can't have."

His eyes darkened slightly. "Who says you can't have them?"

Before I could think of a clever response, someone knocked at the door.

"Meira?" Elder Muriel's voice called through the door. "Are you home, dear?"

Calder and I looked at each other, the moment shattered. He stood quickly.

"Back door?" I whispered.

He nodded, already moving toward the kitchen. "Think about what I said," he murmured as he passed. "About the trips."

I waited until I heard the soft click of the back door before calling out, "Just a moment!" I smoothed my hair and opened the front door to find Elder Muriel standing there with a covered basket.

"There you are, dear," she said warmly. "I hope you're feeling up to visitors?"

"Of course. Please, sit."

She settled into the chair Calder had vacated, smoothing her skirts. I wondered if she could tell he'd been here. "I brought you some of my honey cakes. Thought you might need the strength."

"Strength for what?"

"Well, dear, that's what I came to discuss." Her smile was kind but determined. "The Council has been in discussion for awhile, and we feel it's time to move forward with finding you a suitable partner."

My stomach dropped. "I see."

"We've identified several promising candidates from good

families. Males with strong magic who we believe could complement your abilities." She reached into her basket and withdrew a folded paper. "The rest of the Council doesn't know I'm here, but I thought you might like to review the list before we arrange formal meetings. I would if it were me."

I took the paper with numb fingers. "Formal meetings?"

"Opportunities to get to know them better. Perhaps share a meal, take a walk, see if there's any compatibility." She stood, patting my shoulder. "Take the next day or so to look them over, and we'll formalize it in front of the rest of the Council. If you choose not to accept a partner," she hesitated. "Well, I suppose we'll need to know that too."

After she left, I sat staring at the list in my hands, my heart pounding. Five names. Five potential husbands were chosen without any input from me.

Calder hadn't meant to be cruel—but it still hurt, the way he'd made me believe it was safe to want something more. *Who says you can't have them?*

THE NEXT MORNING, Aoife arrived with her healer's bag and settled into the chair across the table from me without her usual pleasantries.

"How are you feeling?" she asked, settling into the chair across from me.

"Better. Calder stopped by yesterday to check on me."

"Hmm."

I studied her face. "You knew I was outside your cottage the other day, didn't you?"

"I wondered how long it would take you to confess." She pulled out a small glass bottle and set it on the table. "You left rather quickly."

"I heard enough."

"Apparently not enough to do anything about it." Her tone was mild, but pointed.

"Why is he worried about me?"

She turned slowly, still holding a jar of dried white petals in one hand. A wicked smile bloomed across her face, she'd just been waiting for me to say something first.

"Why does he care?"

She crossed to me, placing one warm hand on my forehead and cupping my face with the other. She hummed the same sound that had comforted me through countless childhood scrapes. "You're getting better," she said finally. "Much better than I expected."

"And?" I asked.

"You can go back to the shop, but only on light duty. I still don't want you using any magic until the day after tomorrow. If you insist on walking the wards, take someone with you. I don't want you too far from home alone."

"Should I take Calder with me?" I asked, sharper than I meant to.

"If you'd like."

I looked down at my hands, trying to find the right words. "Aoife... the Council is going to force me into a partnership." I pulled out Muriel's list and handed it to her. "The Council wants me to choose a husband from this."

Aoife scanned the paper, her expression darkening. "Nolan Fletcher is on here."

"Third from the top."

"That boy is a snake." She set the list aside. "What did you tell Muriel?"

"Nothing yet. She wants an answer in a few days, and if I refuse, they'll replace me entirely."

"So don't refuse," she said simply.

I blinked. "What?"

"Don't refuse their choice. Make your own." Her smile turned wicked. "Beat them to it."

"I can't just—" I started, but she cut me off.

"Why not? You heard that boy when you were eavesdropping through the windows. He's worried sick about you. He's not sleeping because he cares about you. When's the last time someone lost sleep over you, Meira?"

Never, that I knew of. "But he's just being kind—"

"Kindness doesn't keep you awake at night," Aoife said firmly. "Fear does. Love does. The kind of love that gets under your skin and makes you do foolish things like organize guard patrols and carry unconscious girls across entire villages."

My heart might beat through my chest. "You think he...?"

"I think that boy would move mountains for you if you'd let him, but I think you're too afraid to try. What's the worst that could happen? He says no, and you're right back where you started, and facing an arranged partnership you don't want." She reached across and squeezed my hand. "Stop being afraid of what you want, Meira. Let yourself reach for something that makes you happy."

"What if he says no?"

"What if he says yes?" She stood, shouldering her bag.

"The Council wants me partnered," I said slowly, the idea taking root. "They never specified it had to be with someone they chose."

"Now you're thinking like a smart girl." Aoife grinned as she gathered her things to leave. "Though I'd move quickly if I were you. These things have a way of getting decided for us if we wait too long."

I sat holding Muriel's list, thinking about Calder's stories and the way he'd looked at me.

Who says you can't have them?

Maybe it was time to find out.

7

———

I was halfway out the door, still pinning my hair back, rehearsing the most outrageous question I'd ever planned to ask someone.

Will you lie to the Council for me? Tell them we're courting so they can't marry me off to someone else?

Calder would probably laugh. Or worse, say yes without hesitation because it wouldn't mean anything to him. When to me, it already *did*. But I had to ask. I was going to ask. I was—

Three urgent knocks at the door made it shake in its frame.

I opened it, expecting Brenna, maybe even Aoife had come back to scold me for taking too long to get to Calder's.

Instead, Nolan Fletcher stood on my porch, looking far too pleased with himself.

"The Elder Council requests your presence," he said smoothly. "Immediately."

My stomach dropped. "It has to be now?"

His smile widened. "They've sent me to escort you." He offered me his arm as if he were doing me a favor.

"I'm perfectly capable of walking to the Council Chamber."

"Of course you are," he agreed quickly. "But after what

happened at the wedding...it's better to be cautious. I'd feel terrible if something happened on my watch."

I shut the door in his face.

I braided my hair three times before it laid the way I wanted. Through the window, I watched him pace on my porch, looking more irritated by the second.

Good.

The walk to the Council Chamber felt like being led to the gallows.

Nolan chattered the whole way about village matters and his family's long service to Glenmere, like I gave a shit. I barely heard him, I was too focused on the knot growing in my stomach.

All four elders, Thomas, Muriel, Lena and James were already seated when we arrived, arranged in their high-backed chairs like thrones. A single, smaller, chair sat in the center for me. A not-so-subtle reminder of who held the power, forcing whoever was in it to look up when addressing the Council.

"Ah, Meira," Elder Lena said as we entered. "Thank you for coming. How are you feeling?"

"Better," I said as I took my seat, hands clasped to hide their trembling.

"Are you?" Elder Thomas raised an eyebrow. "Because we've noticed something interesting. The wards haven't been neglected in your absence."

"Someone with considerable skill has been tending them," Elder Muriel continued. "It's almost as if you haven't stopped working."

Calder was watching the wards, looking out for threats, but nobody had been *working* on them as far as I knew.

"The wards are holding, that's what matters."

"What matters," Elder Thomas snapped, "is that you collapsed at a public event. That you're draining yourself to the point of unconsciousness."

"I appreciate your concern," I said carefully, "but I'm capable of—"

"The Council has reached a decision," Elder Thomas interrupted. "We've been discussing this amongst ourselves for months, but recent events have made action necessary. You must take a partner if you want to remain in your position."

"And if I refuse?" I asked, even though I already knew the answer.

"Then the Council will find someone new. Perhaps whoever is working on them now." It was the first time Elder James had spoken, but his message was clear.

Elder Muriel nodded, her expression sympathetic but firm. "We've identified several young males from good valley families that we believe possess magic that could complement your own."

Gods forbid someone without the proper bloodline possess complementary magic.

"We've prepared a list for you," Elder Thomas said, retrieving a piece of folded parchment from his robe. "We suggest you meet with each of them over the coming weeks to determine compatibility. Both magical and... personal."

"And if I find none of them suitable?" I asked, though I already knew the answer.

"Then the Council will make the choice for you," Elder Thomas said, his voice flat. "This isn't just about you, Meira. It's about the safety of everyone in this valley."

"I see," I said, struggling to keep my voice steady. "And how long do I have to interview these candidates?"

"The new moon," Elder Thomas said. "Two weeks from tomorrow."

Unless Calder agreed, if I ever got the chance to ask him, I'd have two weeks until I lost the independence I'd fought so hard to maintain.

"We have invited the candidates here today," Elder Muriel added, "so you can be properly introduced."

My head snapped up. "Today? Now?" She hadn't said anything about this when she brought me the list.

She smiled as if this were a wonderful surprise instead of an ambush. "They're waiting outside. We thought it best not to waste time."

Before I could protest, the doors opened and five males filed in.

I recognized all of them, of course—our village wasn't large enough for strangers. Tully, the baker's son, looked as if he'd rather be anywhere else, flour still dusting the cuffs of his shirt. Good—that made two of us. Finn, one of Conor's friends, gave me a sympathetic smile. I knew Finn had to be a good male at least, Conor wouldn't keep company that wasn't. The others gazed around the Council Chamber with appropriate horror, except for Nolan, who stared directly at me with fiery ambition in his eyes.

His dark hair was combed back, and he was dressed in finer clothes than the rest of the group. He stood a step in front of the other males, like he thought this was already his.

"Gentlemen," Elder Thomas began, "you understand why you're here. Meira needs a suitable partner for the wardcraft. Each of you has demonstrated the proper—"

The door opened again.

Every head turned as Calder stepped into the chamber, his shoulders tense and his jaw clenched.

What the hell was he doing here?

His usual composure had slipped, enough that I could see worry in the crease between his brows as he scanned every face in the chamber. When his gaze found mine, some of that tension eased from his shoulders, the furrow in his brow smoothing slightly.

"I apologize for the interruption," he said, voice carrying

easily through the chamber. "But I heard this meeting was about the wards."

Elder Thomas frowned but couldn't hide a touch of deference. "Mr. Byrne. This is a closed session."

"I understand that sir," Calder nodded politely. "But I believe I have information relevant to your discussion. About the ward tampering I discovered."

Several people gasped. Even Nolan looked startled.

"Tampering?" Elder Thomas leaned forward. "What kind of tampering?"

"Someone has been systematically weakening the ward structure," Calder explained. "I noticed it while checking the wards this morning."

"You've been looking after the wards?" Elder Thomas asked.

"In addition to the voluntary patrols, yes. I thought Meira should be able to rest without worry."

My face burned, I hadn't been to the wards in days.

"This only proves what we've all been thinking," Nolan jumped in eagerly. "Meira clearly needs immediate support. A proper partner would have caught this earlier."

Shit. If Calder's information about the tampering hadn't made me look incompetent, surely Nolan's comment solidified the Council's decision.

I'd failed at the wards the very first day I'd been in charge, and Calder had rescued me then too.

I looked at the list crumpled in my hand, at Nolan's triumphant face, at the Council's expectant gazes, and something snapped.

I couldn't choose between these candidates. I couldn't let Elder Thomas, and Nolan, win by default. I'd rather live a lie than let anyone else decide who I was.

The words were out before I could stop them.

"You're right," I said, standing. "I do need a partner."

Every eye in the room was fixed on me.

"Which is why I'm happy to announce that Calder and I have already established a courtship."

Silence fell over the chamber.

Calder's eyebrows rose—the only sign of surprise on his otherwise composed face. Around the room though, mouths fell open.

"Calder and I," I continued, the lie tumbling out faster, "We've been seeing each other. For a while now."

"Ridiculous!" Nolan sputtered.

"We've been discreet," I insisted, praying Calder would play along. "When it happened, it happened suddenly, and we wanted some time for it to just be ours. I've been teaching him about the wards, and he's been helping me."

Elder Thomas turned to Calder. "Is this true?"

I held my breath, one word from him, and this shield protecting my freedom would shatter.

Calder moved across the chamber to stand beside me, close enough that I felt the heat from his body against my skin.

"Our magics recognize each other," he said simply.

He hadn't answered the question, but no one fought him on it, so I stood a little straighter and acted as though he had.

"Among my people," Calder said carefully, "we recognize when certain magics align. It's not something we choose—it simply is. When that happens, we don't call it courting. We call it recognition."

He paused. "It means the potential for a bond already exists. The compatibility itself isn't binding, but if we choose to honor it, it has a way of becoming something more."

I kept my face neutral, even when I could feel the heat bloom across my cheeks as I remembered he couldn't lie.

He couldn't lie.

He couldn't lie.

Elder Muriel leaned forward, eyes sharp with interest. "Like something from before the divide?"

"I believe it's possible," Calder said. "Before there were valley fae or forest fae, there were just fae. The separation is recent, in the long memory of magic."

"This changes nothing!" Nolan protested. "We need valley-born fae for valley wards!"

But Elder Thomas was no longer looking at Nolan. He was watching us. "If their magics are already compatible, as claimed..."

My heart pounded. The trap I'd set was already closing, and I'd walked into it willingly.

"Are you both prepared to formalize this arrangement?" Elder Thomas asked.

Calder brushed his hand over mine in silent offering. I laced my fingers with his.

I met his eyes, and found only gentle kindness.

"Of course," I managed, the same time he said, "Yes."

"Then this matter is settled," Elder Muriel declared before anyone could protest further. "We'll have a handfasting ceremony."

A handfasting. One of our oldest traditions, where couples stood before the village while their hands were bound together with a braided cord. It wasn't marriage, yet, but still a formal and public promise. We would be expected to share a home, make decisions together, and be seen as partners in all things.

A year ago, I couldn't look Calder in the eye. Now I was agreeing to bind my life to his.

"But not today," I blurted. "Sorcha isn't back from her honeymoon. She would kill me if she wasn't here for it."

A few elders chuckled. Even Thomas cracked a smile.

"Very well," Muriel said. "We'll give you some time to plan with Sorcha."

As the chamber emptied, Nolan stormed out first, his face twisted with silent fury. The other candidates followed with expressions ranging from disappointment to outright relief.

Elder Muriel gave us an encouraging nod as she gathered her papers. "We'll speak more about the ceremony details soon," she said, turning to go. The door clicked shut behind her.

And then it was just us.

"That was bold," he said, eyes still on me. "Even for you."

There was no anger in his face.

"You do realize," he said, voice low, "that we just declared a bond older than the village of Glenmere."

This time when he smiled, it wasn't reassuring—it was conspiratorial. It was the kind of smile that said he knew exactly what I'd done, exactly the situation I'd put us in, and that he was going to help me do it anyway.

I nodded, but I didn't know what he meant by that, or everything I'd just agreed to. What *we'd* just agreed to.

Our hands were still intertwined as we left the Council Chamber, and it felt both protective and possessive. Outside, villagers in the square stopped their conversations to stare.

Maybe I should have pulled my hand away. Maybe we should have established some boundaries before we stepped into public view, but the warmth of his palm against mine brought me some much appreciated comfort as whispers spread throughout the market stalls. And when his thumb brushed across my knuckles, so light that I might have imagined it, something in me settled.

Whatever this was between us, my magic knew his. And his knew mine.

And that terrified me more than anything the Council could threaten.

8

———————

We didn't get very far before it started to rain, hard, but neither of us changed our pace.

His hand stayed wrapped around mine, steady and warm. I wondered if he'd forgotten he was still holding my hand, or if he'd never intended to stop.

When the road split—one path toward my cottage, the other trailing off toward the edge of the village—I slowed. Calder noticed, his pace adjusting with mine. He glanced over, rain slipping down the side of his face. "My place is closer," he said quietly. "If you want to talk."

I looked at him then, at the way the rain had curled the ends of his hair. I watched the way his thumb brushed across my knuckles, and again, I wondered if he didn't realize he was doing it. I gave a slight nod, and kept walking towards his home, as he fell into step beside me.

The building sat at the edge of the village where the neatly arranged cottages gave way to wilder growth. Unlike the white-washed stone walls and thatched roofs of valley dwellings, his workshop was built of dark, rough-hewn timber and moss-covered stone with a slate roof. It didn't look built so much as rooted—like the woods had made room for him and he'd simply settled into the hollow they left behind.

By the time we reached the porch, my sleeves were soaked and cold had crept down beneath my collar. I didn't care.

Calder opened the door and stepped inside, still holding my hand until we were both through. The air inside was warmer, and a fire burned low near the entry, just enough to take the edge off the chill.

We paused just inside the threshold and stepped out of our wet shoes, where mine made an unfortunate squelch. The space was warm and surprisingly tidy, with a workbench running along one wall, tools hung in clean rows, and shelves held jars of materials labeled in neat handwriting. A fire burned in a stone hearth, casting the single room in warm light.

The stone floor at the entry was cool beneath my feet. Calder moved both pairs onto the stone hearth, and gave a small nod toward the other room.

"The fire's better in here," he said. "You can warm up. I'll grab a towel."

I followed him through a wide doorway and into what had to be the house proper. The room was simple but inviting. A woven rug stretched across dark wooden floors. A soft-looking couch faced a much larger hearth, where the fire burned low but steady. Off to the side, a narrow kitchen held a small table, two chairs, and a window that faced the forest trees, half-fogged from the weather.

I moved closer to the fire and crouched down, rubbing my hands together. I heard him moving through the hall, a cabinet opening, the quiet creak of old hinges.

When he returned, he had a towel draped over one arm, and one of his tunics in his hand. He held it out to me, it looked soft, and oversized.

"I should've walked you home first," he said. "Let you change into something dry. I wasn't thinking."

I shrugged. I hadn't been thinking too much either.

He hesitated, then gave a small, almost embarrassed shake of his head. "I just didn't want to let go yet."

I felt a small smile tug at my lips. I took the towel from him, then the shirt.

"There's a bathroom down the hall on the left, or my bedroom is at the end of the hall if you wanted to change."

"Thank you," I said and nodded.

The door to his bedroom stood open, and I slipped inside with the towel in one hand, the shirt in the other. The room was simple, the bed took up most of the space, and a plain wooden chair stood near the dresser. A few books were stacked beside the bed, not arranged, just placed wherever they landed.

I used the towel first, running it along my arms, across my shoulders, then carefully through the ends of my hair. The fabric was rough but warm. My clothes were soaked through, clinging and heavy, so I stripped them off piece by piece and wrung them out over the towel. Then I draped them over the back of the chair and reached for the shirt he'd given me.

It was oversized, clearly meant for someone with twice my width and a full foot of additional height. The sleeves hung long, the hem falling low over my thighs. But it was dry, soft against my skin, and still carried some trace of the fire-lit room outside. I pulled it over my head and adjusted the sleeves, then caught sight of myself in the mirror above the dresser.

The shirt covered everything, but it still felt intimate. I considered looking for a blanket to throw around my waist just in case, an added layer of comfort, but decided against it. The shirt fit the way it fit. I was warm enough.

I squared my shoulders, took one last breath to settle the weird flutter that had started low in my belly, and opened the door.

I stepped back into the living room, carrying my wet clothes and walked through the low orange glow the fire was casting across the floor. I draped the clothes over the back of a wooden chair he'd placed near the fire. Calder had settled on the couch, one ankle resting loosely over his knee, a mug cradled in his hands. He looked up when I entered, and I watched him lose his train of thought. His eyes dropped to his shirt on me, then back up, and he cleared his throat like he'd been caught doing something he shouldn't.

I did a little spin. "What do you think?"

He choked on his tea.

He reached behind him for the blanket draped over the back of the couch and set it beside him on the cushion. I appreciated that silent offering, like he trusted I'd take it if I wanted to.

I laughed. "For my benefit or yours?"

His jaw tightened.

I curled up at the other end of the couch, legs tucked beneath me, the hem of Calder's shirt slipping higher than I'd expected. I adjusted it without thinking, then stopped. I was covered, fully, but I still felt naked somehow.

Calder went into the kitchen and poured a second mug. I tried to focus on the rain tapping against the windows, the crackle of the fire—but all I could see was the line of his shoulders as he moved, the muscle in his arm when he reached for the kettle.

"Do you want honey?" he called, without turning around.

"Yes, please," I said, surprised by how steady my voice sounded.

He brought it over a moment later, warm and just sweet enough. I took it from him carefully, my fingers brushing his.

I cradled my own warm mug in my hands, and tried not to read into every moment of silence between us. I tried not to wonder what he was thinking. If I thought about it too long, I'd convince myself he was regretting it, all of this, and that maybe he didn't know how to tell me.

I couldn't sit with that.

"They were going to force me to court Nolan," I said suddenly, the words sharp against the quiet. "I didn't know what else to do. I'm sorry," I said, quieter now. "I shouldn't have dragged you into this."

He blinked, then a smile tugged at the corner of his mouth. "You did catch me off guard. But it's understandable." He let the smile spread fully across his face now. "No one should be forced to endure Nolan."

I laughed despite myself, some of the tension draining from my shoulders. "Still, I should have asked first."

"Would you have?" He raised an eyebrow. "Asked me, I mean. If you'd had time to think about it."

"Probably not," I admitted. I tried to make it sound light, like a joke.

"Then I suppose it worked out," he said, but he wasn't looking at me anymore. His gaze had shifted past me, toward the hearth. "Sometimes the best decisions are the ones we don't overthink."

"Why are you agreeing to this? What do you get out of it?"

Calder leaned forward, elbows on his knees. "Access to the wards, for one thing."

"Why do you want access to the wards?"

"I've been studying ward systems for years," he said. "Valley wards are different from forest protections. I've been curious about them since I arrived."

It was a reasonable enough explanation, but there was still something guarded in his tone. "So...just an academic interest then?"

He shrugged one shoulder. "Is that so hard to believe?"

"Yes," I said bluntly.

He huffed a soft laugh, and almost smiled. "I love how you say exactly what you're thinking. The wards and exploring our compatibility. I'd like to see what we're capable of."

"The connection between our magic, like at the wedding rehearsal? You could feel that?"

His expression turned serious. "Yes," he said simply. "I felt it."

A silence fell between us, broken only by the crackling of the fire.

"And the living together part?"

He looked up. "What about it?"

"I know it's tradition after a handfasting. People will expect it."

"They might expect it," Calder said gently. "But it's not a rule. We do this how *you* want to do it."

The knot in my stomach eased a little.

"How long do you think we'll be able to keep this up?" he asked quietly, his eyes fixed on the flames.

I hadn't thought that far ahead. The way he asked worried me, was he already trying to get out of it? "I don't know. Until the elders are convinced, I suppose. Or until..."

"Until you find a real partner?" he suggested.

My chest twisted and tightened. "My parents had something special," I said, unable to keep the edge from my voice. "They were true partners in every sense. The way they worked together, the way they—" I swallowed hard, surprised by the sudden flood of memories. "They could weave enchantments together without speaking. When they worked on the wards together, it was a dance. Yes, sometimes even actual dancing, like the work was effortless."

A tear rolled down my cheek, but I smiled at the memory. "Every morning he'd hum this ridiculous song while he made tea. My mother would roll her eyes, kiss his cheek, and hum the next line under her breath."

I realized this was the first time I'd brought them up unprompted, with anyone, since they passed. It felt like no small thing that it was with Calder.

"Their wardwork is what everyone remembers, but they were so much more than their magic together.

"When I was little, I'd watch them from my window upstairs sometimes. They'd be in the garden, tilling soil or pulling weeds, but it never looked like a chore. Every single thing they did together looked like they were having so much fun. That's what real love, real partnership looks like. Two people, who make even the most boring things beautiful, just by doing them together." I couldn't help but grin as I wiped the tears out of my eyes.

"I don't expect to find that," I said.

I glanced at Calder. "Have you ever heard that the fae were made from stars?"

He nodded.

"My dad used to say he and my mom were made of the same dust." I smiled, the memory warm enough to soothe the ache in my chest. "The first time I asked what he meant, he said, 'Like the gods shaped them from the same star, the same handful of stardust, and laced their bones with the memory of it.'"

Calder didn't say anything.

Binding him to me in a fake courtship hadn't scared him off but maybe monologuing about my dead parents was crossing the line.

When he finally spoke, his voice was gentle. "They sound incredible."

"They were." It felt good to talk about them. For someone to listen. "I'm sorry, I don't usually—"

"Don't apologize," he said softly. "Your memories of them deserve to be shared"

"Well," I said, "thank you for letting me ramble about them anyway."

"It's not rambling," he said, his eyes warm as he gave me a crooked smile.

"We'll figure this thing out together." He paused. "And someday, when you find someone worthy of that kind of partnership..." He looked away. "I'll think of this exact moment and smile knowing how incredible they must be too."

I was the one to break eye contact. I had to look away from the sincerity in his eyes. "You're very good at this," I said, and let out a soft laugh, hoping to lighten the moment.

He stilled. His jaw shifted once, like he was chewing over whether or not to answer. "At what?"

"Playing the part. Being charming." I gestured between us. "This. Making me feel..." I wasn't quite sure how to finish that thought. "Comfortable, I suppose."

He was quiet for a moment, and when I glanced back, his expression was thoughtful. "Maybe we're both better at this than we expected to be."

He stood, offered me a hand. I took it.

"When should we make our first intentional public appearance?"

"Well, I've been told I'm not allowed to walk the wards without you anymore, and I need to go to the market sometime this week," I said. "What if we walked the perimeter in the morning and plan some shopping in a few days? The market would be a good place to run into just about everyone, and there's lots of things to look at if we run out of things to say."

"Perfect."

I stood too, tugging the hem of his shirt lower on my thighs as I moved. "I should probably change." I gathered my clothes from the chair near the fire. They were still damp in places, heavy in my arms. I didn't exactly want to put them back on.

He watched me for a beat. "Don't worry about it," he said, quieter now. "It looks better on you anyway."

I startled a little laugh, shaking my head. "I can't exactly walk home in it. What would the neighbors think?"

He lifted an eyebrow. "It's dark. Let them wonder."

I stared at him, and his smile turned wicked. "Though if Mrs. Blackwood sees you in that, she'll assume we've already consummated."

I burst out laughing, I couldn't help it. I pulled the shirt down a little more, out of habit now. "Well, I guess I'd better walk fast."

Calder chuckled under his breath. "Good luck with that."

I should've headed for the door, but I hesitated for a moment. Because for a second, I could imagine myself staying, even just for a little longer. Maybe until the fire burned down.

Instead, I slipped into my shoes and said, "See you tomorrow morning."

I could feel him hesitating too, just slightly. I thought there might be something else he wanted to say, but he just nodded, and opened the door for me.

It had finally stopped raining, though the air outside was damp and chilly. I didn't look back as I walked down the porch and onto the cobblestones. I was afraid if I did, I'd never make it home.

9

———

It had been three days since that rainy evening I left Calder's wearing his shirt. Three mornings of walking the wards together since then.Three days of comfortable quiet—of watching him work with calm focus and hands that always seemed to know exactly what to do.

The first morning, I'd watched him rest his fingers against one of the wardstones—fingertips first, as he splayed his hands out until both palms were flat to the stone. It looked like he was giving the stone time to recognize him.

It was exactly how my father used to approach the stones. I told him so, before I could think better of it.

Calder had stilled for a moment. His mouth twitched, and I thought he might say something. But he only adjusted his stance, and kept working. I wondered if bringing up my parents so often made him uncomfortable. Or if he just didn't want to break his concentration.

Aoife had insisted I limit my use of magic—only light work, small things. I was allowed just enough to keep the threads active, and enough to let my magic mingle with Calder's.

He never told me to stop, or said I was doing too much. Instead, he'd be the one to pull back, and I followed.

I liked that he didn't coddle me, didn't draw attention to the moments my power faltered.

Still, there were moments I watched him place his hands against stones and the magic flowed from him with such ease, I felt something sharp twist under my ribs. It wasn't quite envy, but an ache of seeing someone slip so easily into this thing I had to work so hard for.

By the third day, I knew his rhythms. I noticed the way he cocked his head when the currents shifted. The way his brow furrowed as he adjusted a seam in the southern marker, I wondered if he was able to see the wards more clearly than I ever had.

And this morning when I slipped on a mossy stone near the western boundary, he caught me with one hand at my waist, steady and instinctive, like he'd already known I'd need him there. I'd come home with dirt still covering my palms, but it wasn't the fall I kept thinking about. It was how, for the second time now, he hadn't let me hit the ground.

He walked me home like usual, but instead of heading to the shop, I bathed to remove any trace of moss or mud, and got ready.

Because today, we were going to the market. Together. Our first planned public appearance as a supposedly courting couple.

I stood in front of my wardrobe for the third time, having already discarded two perfectly reasonable outfits.

IT WAS JUST THE MARKET, I reminded myself. *With Calder.*

But even after days of private familiarity, my nerves were a mess.

I finally settled on a simple blue dress. It wasn't anything special, but my mother had always said it brought out my eyes.

I smoothed my hands over the fabric, trying to quiet the flutter in my chest.

The knock at my door sent my heart jumping into my throat. I took a steadying breath, forcing my fingers to stop trembling as I reached for the handle.

And there he was.

Calder stood like a mountain in my doorway, the morning sun catching in his dark hair and gilding his skin with gold. He'd made an effort today—his usual sawdust-covered work clothes replaced by a dark green shirt that made the gold flecks in his eyes more pronounced. I'd always known he was handsome, but this was distracting.

"Ready?" he asked, and offered his arm.

"As I'll ever be," I muttered, sliding my hand into the crook of his elbow.

I didn't hesitate taking his arm, not after the last few days we'd spent together. The now-familiar pulse of our magic meeting rippled through me like a stone dropped in still water.

"You look nice," he said as we started down the path toward the village center.

I glanced up at him, trying to decipher his tone. I was wretched at accepting compliments, but by the way he looked at me made this one feel safe to accept.

"Thank you," I said finally. "You clean up well yourself."

That was an understatement. The breadth of his shoulders was impossible to ignore in a shirt that was more fitted than his usual work clothes. There was something about seeing him dressed like this that made every part of him more noticeable. Too noticeable.

"Do you think this will be enough?" I asked, voice softer than I intended as we reached the market square. "To convince them?"

He glanced around, letting his mouth quirk up into a small smile. "Depends on who you're trying to convince."

"Looks like...everyone." I could already feel half the market staring, and we hadn't even reached the first stall. "Word must travel fast."

"Then I suppose we'd better put on a good show." His voice dropped lower, just for me, and he covered my hand on his arm with his own.

The warmth of his palm shot through me like Aoife's strongest reviving tea, but infinitely more pleasant. My magic surged up beneath my skin to meet his touch, eager and responsive, like a cat arching into a caress.

The market square sprawled before us in a riot of color and noise. Tables groaned under piles of fresh produce, glassware caught the morning light in dazzling prisms, and fabrics fluttered in the breeze like butterfly wings. At the center of it all, a group of village children danced to the music of a musician's fiddle.

"What's on your list?" Calder asked, navigating us through the crowd with a grace that should've been impossible for someone his size.

As he guided me through a crowded section of the market, his hand found the small of my back. The gentle pressure of his touch was casual, protective even, but that didn't slow my pulse.

"Just some herbs and kitchen supplies," I said, trying to focus on my shopping list. "Nothing exciting."

We moved from stall to stall, gathering what I needed. When my arms grew full, Calder simply took everything without comment, carrying my things, as if shopping together was something we always did.

I pretended not to notice the way the older women paused their haggling to glance our way. Or the knowing nod Mrs. Fennelly gave me from behind her yarn stand, like she'd been waiting for this moment all along. I told myself it didn't mean anything, but I couldn't deny that I liked being seen like this with him. I liked feeling as if being next to him was somewhere I belonged.

At the herb stall, I was examining bundles of lavender when Calder leaned over my shoulder to look at the selection, his chest briefly pressing against my back as he reached past me to touch a bunch of dried rosemary.

"This would pair well with the honey from your pantry," he murmured, his breath warm against my ear.

I froze, caught between the urge to step away and the unexpected desire to lean back into his solid warmth. "How do you know what's in my pantry?"

My mind told me to move, but my body stayed rooted. My magic surged again, like it had been waiting for this exact contact.

His laugh rumbled through his chest, and where it touched my back, through me. "My mother used to make these rosemary honey scones and ugh," he groaned at the memory and I felt that sound all the way to my toes. "You've never had anything better in your life."

I turned, intending to create some space between us, only to find myself facing him directly, much closer than I'd anticipated. His eyes widened slightly, pupils dilating as his gaze dropped briefly to my mouth before returning to meet mine.

For one suspended moment, neither of us moved. The market noise receded, replaced by the sound of my own heartbeat thundering in my ears. His expression shifted, something hungry and intent replacing his usual careful composure.

"Meira! Calder!"

Hearing our names fractured the moment, and we broke apart like guilty teenagers.

I turned to find Sorcha weaving through the crowd toward us, Conor in tow. Her copper hair gleamed in the sunlight, but not nearly as bright as her smile. My stomach dropped. I'd been so distracted, I'd completely forgotten that Sorcha and Conor would be back from their honeymoon trip. And of course she'd heard. Everyone had heard.

"There you are! We've been looking everywhere for you!"

"Sorcha," I managed, suddenly hypcraware of how close Calder stood beside me. "Back from your honeymoon trip already?"

"Just yesterday," she said, enveloping me in a hug that smelled of honeysuckle and home. When she pulled back, her eyes darted between Calder and me with gleeful curiosity. "So it's true then? The two of you?"

Heat flooded my cheeks. "Word travels fast."

"Elder Muriel told my mother, who told half the village by sundown," Sorcha confirmed, eyes sparkling. "I knew something was happening between you two at the wedding!"

"Did you?" I squeaked, caught by surprise.

Conor clapped Calder on the shoulder with the easy familiarity of old friends. "You sneaky bastard! How many times did I try to introduce you to Meira properly? And you were already planning to court her behind my back."

Calder gave a soft huff of laughter and ducked his head, running a hand through his hair.

"I even told him he should just talk to you himself," Conor told me, shaking his head with fond exasperation. "You remember, Calder? After that night at the festival last autumn when Meira lit the grove with floating pumpkins and every kid thought it was the best magic they'd ever seen?"

Calder gave a slow nod, and resigned himself to Conor's teasing, "I remember."

The idea that Conor had offered to introduce Calder to me several times, and that he'd never taken him up on it—felt like a rock in my stomach. Maybe he'd never had an interest in meeting me. If so, with every mess I'd dragged him into, he probably wished he never had met me.

"About time someone broke through that wall she built around herself," Conor added, grinning at me.

"I haven't built a wall," I protested, though the words sounded weak even to my own ears.

"It's more like a fortress," Sorcha corrected, linking her arm through mine and drawing me slightly away from Calder. "With a moat and fire-breathing dragons."

"Knights in turrets, bows at the ready," Conor added.

"Okay, okay!" I rolled my eyes, fighting both a smile and a flush of embarrassment. Was that how people saw me?

Calder watched our exchange with a fond expression. He simply stood there, solid and present, my purchases still cradled in his arms.

"How long has this been going on?" Sorcha demanded in a stage whisper that was about as subtle as a herd of bell-wearing goats at dinner time. "And why didn't you tell me?"

I thought she'd be upset with me when she found out from someone else, but the way she sounded more excited than anything made it worse. This was Sorcha, who had been by my side since we were toddling around the village square together. Sorcha, who had held me through the worst nights after my parents died. Could I really lie to her? I hated thinking she'd be just as heartbroken as I would when this was over.

"It's... complicated," I hedged, unwilling to look her in the eye. "We wanted to be sure before making it public."

"Well, I want details," Sorcha declared, her expression making it clear she wouldn't be satisfied with vague answers for long. "All of them. You must come to dinner tonight—both of you." She raised her voice to include the men in our conversation. "Our place for dinner tonight. No excuses!"

My eyes sought Calder's in panic. A few hours in the market was one thing, but an entire evening of close scrutiny by the person who knew me better than anyone? Sorcha would see through us in moments.

His gaze met mine, steady and reassuring. A slight tilt of his head, a question in his eyes that I somehow understood perfectly: *Can we do this? Should we?*

We had to. I responded with the smallest of nods, surprising myself with how easily we'd fallen into this wordless communication.

"We'd love to," Calder answered for both of us, stepping closer until his arm brushed mine. His hand found the small of my back, and the touch felt more intimate this time.

"Perfect!" Sorcha clapped her hands together. "I'll make that berry tart you love, Meira."

"You don't have to go to any trouble," I said. I hated how earnest she sounded.

"Nonsense! This calls for celebration. My best friend, finally with someone worthy of her." Her gaze softened as she looked between us. "I always hoped you'd let someone in. I'm glad you waited until it was someone who sees you. It's hard to believe you've both been right here this whole time."

"Right here," I echoed through a too-tight smile. "Life's full of surprises."

"Just proves the right timing makes all the difference," Calder said.

Sorcha beamed and gave my arm a last squeeze before she and Conor disappeared into the crowd. As soon as they were out of earshot, I exhaled like I'd been holding my breath underwater.

"Dinner with our closest friends," Calder murmured, and I could hear the faintest thread of anxiety beneath his calm exterior. "That should be interesting."

"Sorcha can be... intense," I warned, the understatement of the century. "She'll want to know everything. And I mean everything. When we first met, how you asked me to court, our first kiss—gods, she'll probably ask how many children we're planning to have."

"Conor is just as bad," Calder said. "Let's hope whatever story we're telling is the same one." His hand was still warm at the small of my back, and I fought the urge to lean into it.

I tried not to think about how natural it felt to have his fingers splayed against my spine, how easily my body curved toward his.

By the time we left the market, my nerves were worn threadbare from the constant awareness of being watched, from the effort of playing a part that my body seemed all too eager to embrace.

We walked back toward my cottage in a silence that could have been awkward but felt comfortable instead. When we reached my door, Calder set down the market purchases and turned to me, his expression thoughtful.

"So, dinner this evening," he confirmed. "I'll come by to walk with you?"

I nodded, even though my heartbeat was already spiking. We'd said goodbye like this at least four other times already, every time he'd walked me home from the wards, but this one felt different.

Maybe it was because most of the village had seen us together now. Maybe it was the dinner with Sorcha looming. Or maybe it was just, the ache of knowing how easily all of it was starting to mean to me.

Calder didn't give me time to overthink. He reached for my hand without hesitation, the calluses on his fingers rough against my skin as he raised my right hand to his lips. His eyes never left mine, not even as he pressed his mouth to my knuckles with a devastating slowness turned a kiss that should have been innocent into something more. It sent heat rushing up my arm, a flush to my cheeks, a pulse of magic so sudden my own leapt to the surface of my skin as if reaching for him.

"Until tonight, then," he said, his voice lower than usual, his eyes never leaving mine.

I tried to form words—any words—but nothing coherent made it past my lips. I nodded, hoping I didn't look as flustered as I felt.

He smiled with his eyes, a small, private thing just for me. Then he turned and walked away, his broad shoulders outlined against the mid-day sun.

I stood there unmoving. My hand still tingled where his lips had touched it, and I rubbed the spot absently, trying to memorize the sensation.

I should've gone inside. Changed. Started planning for tonight. But I couldn't move from the doorway, I just stood there like a fool, breathless and aching.

10

───────

I spent the next several hours in my cottage, mentally rehearsing answers to every possible question Sorcha might throw at us.

When did we realize our feelings? What was our first date like? How soon will we marry? I came up with a dozen different versions of our fictional love story, only to discard each one as too unbelievable or too complicated to remember.

Eventually, I gave up on planning and did what I could control. Which is how I found myself standing in front of my wardrobe again, rummaging through dresses I hadn't worn in years. My fingers brushed against something soft and deep green, tucked toward the back.

It was one of the last dresses my mother made for me. Forest green with golden leaves embroidered around the neckline and cuffs—intricate work that had taken her weeks. "For when you want to feel beautiful," she'd said, tucking a strand of hair behind my ear. I'd never had the heart to wear it.

I fastened the tiny buttons up the back one by one, stretching awkwardly to reach the ones between my shoulder blades. It took longer than it should have, but eventually I managed.

Wearing this dress, I couldn't help feeling like I was crossing some invisible line. I ran my hands over the embroidery, remembering her bent over her work, humming as she stitched.

Would she approve of what I was doing? This deception? Probably not, but I hoped she'd understand the desperation behind it.

I twisted my hair up into something more elegant than my usual practical style, letting a few curls frame my face. Just as I was pinning the last strand in place, a knock sounded at my door.

I pressed my palms against my skirt. Deep breath. Shoulders back.

I opened the door and every thought I'd rehearsed vanished like smoke.

He stood on my doorstep, completely filling the frame, holding a package wrapped in brown paper. He looked better than he had any right to—grounded and quietly handsome, in the way he always was.

But it was his expression that undid me completely. When his eyes found mine, they widened, his lips parting slightly as his gaze traveled over me in a slow, deliberate assessment that felt like a physical touch.

"Meira," he said, and just my name in that deep voice made something low in my stomach tighten. "You look..."

I braced myself for a polite compliment, something appropriate for our charade.

"Beautiful," he finished, his voice roughened at the edges. "Absolutely beautiful."

It wasn't the words themselves—I'd been called beautiful before—but the raw sincerity in his voice that caught me off guard.

"Thank you," I managed. "You look... nice too."

A smile tugged at the corner of his mouth, and I swear his eyes sparkled. "High praise indeed."

I rolled my eyes, desperately grateful for the return to our more casual dynamic. "What's that?" I gestured to the package he carried.

"A gift for our hosts," he explained, shifting to reveal a bottle of wine in his other hand. "Wine from my personal stores, and —" He unwrapped the brown paper to reveal a wooden box.

It was about the size of a jewelry box, its lid adorned with intertwining vines and flowers carved with such precision they almost seemed to move in the fading light. The wood itself had a warm, golden glow that no stain could achieve—this was the natural beauty of the material, coaxed out by skilled hands.

"Calder," I breathed, unable to hide my wonder. "It's beautiful."

"It's a memory box," he explained. "A bit of a tradition in my family. It's a common gift when a couple establishes a home together. Every year, on the same day, the couple adds a note inside—something they want to remember from that year. It could be anything, a favorite moment, a promise, a wish for the year to come."

I looked closer and noticed that the box had two keyholes on opposite sides. "How does it work?"

"Each person has a key, and the box only opens when both are turned at the same time," he explained.

He'd carved this with his own hands, and something about that knocked the wind out of me.

Not just the craftsmanship or the sentiment—though both were enough.

It was the fact that Calder Byrne, who barely spoke unless he meant it, had put time and care into something like this. And that it was for Sorcha made it hurt worse, somehow, maybe because she was the closest thing I had to family. In making this, he'd peeled back a piece of himself and handed it over. And the act alone was enough to leave my own heart exposed.

"That's a lovely tradition," I said, swallowing past the lump in my throat. I kept my hands at my sides, afraid if I touched the box again, I'd say something stupid.

"I had hoped to have it finished before their wedding, but I doubt they'll mind," he said.

"It's perfect," I said, my voice steadier than I felt. "We should go before Sorcha collects us herself."

The walk to Sorcha and Conor's cottage took us through the center of the village, with plenty of eyes on us. Calder offered his arm, and I took it without thinking. The magic stirred between us—familiar now, steady. It didn't rattle me anymore. If anything, I missed it when it wasn't there.

"Are you ready for this?" he asked quietly as we approached their door.

"No," I admitted, fighting the urge to smooth my dress for the hundredth time. "Sorcha knows me better than anyone. If anyone will see through us, it's her."

"Then we'll just have to be convincing." He covered my hand on his arm with his own, and the warmth of his palm seeped through me like honey, sweet and golden.

For once, instead of shying away, I let myself feel it. If we were pretending, then I decided I was at least allowed to enjoy it.

11

———

The door flew open before we could knock, revealing Sorcha with her copper hair piled atop her head and a wide smile on her face.

"Finally!" she said, and pulled me into a hug before wrapping her arms around Calder as well. "Come in, come in! Conor's just finishing up in the kitchen."

Their cottage was small and warm, filled with mismatched furniture and the kind of clutter that only grows with time. The table was already set with ceramic dishes, candles flickering in the windows. It already felt like a home, and it made my chest ache.

"We brought gifts," Calder said, setting the bottle of wine and the box on the table.

Sorcha peeled away the brown wrapping and smiled, fingers trailing over the carvings. "You show-off," she said, swatting his arm. "It's beautiful."

She turned it over in her hands and called for Conor, and together they tested the twin keys. The lid opened with a soft click, revealing velvet lining inside.

"I love it, Calder. Thank you," she said. She set the box on the mantle, where it looked right at home.

Conor poured the wine at the table, while Sorcha disappeared into the kitchen, working in tandem like they did this all the time.

I started to follow, but she waved me off.

Calder and I ended up on the couch together, where he placed his arm around my shoulders.

Sorcha announced that dinner was ready, with a spread that made my mouth water—roasted game hen with herbs, golden potatoes, fresh bread still warm from the oven, and vegetables from their garden. And true to her word, my favorite berry tart waited on the sideboard, its crust perfectly browned and glistening with sugar.

"This smells amazing Sorcha" I said as we all settled around the table. "You really didn't have to go through all of this trouble."

"Only the best for my oldest friend and her future husband," Sorcha replied with a wink. "So you two finally stopped pretending not to notice each other," Conor said, grinning as we filled our plates. "Took you long enough."

I shot a panicked glance at Calder, but his expression remained calm, his voice smooth when he replied.

"I think I've always noticed Meira," he said. "Remember when I first moved to the village, and had that trouble with the roof on my workshop?"

About a month after Calder had arrived in Glenmere, a spring storm had damaged several buildings in the village, including his newly established workshop. It was going to be a couple of days before Conor could get to the repairs, and he had asked if I could put charms over the damage to offer some protection until he could get it fixed. I remembered feeling a bit smug about helping Calder after our non-encounter on his first day here.

"I tried to set you up with her then," Conor said.

"It didn't feel like the right time," Calder said without looking at me. "She had a lot on her plate with her shop and having just taken over the wards," he went on, his thumb tracing small circles against his wineglass. "And I was still settling in, learning my place here."

I listened intently when Calder spoke, assuming he'd have to avoid any false details. "So love at first sight for you?" Sorcha asked.

"When she collapsed at the wedding—" he said, his voice softening, "it scared me. I didn't sleep that night, I just paced and waited to find out if she was okay." He trailed off, shaking his head. "All I thought about that night was what if I'd lost her before I'd even had a chance to know her?"

He reached for me and laced his fingers with mine. It felt like something he did all the time.

He didn't answer the question, not really, but of all the things he did say... They had to be true.

"What about you, Meira?" Sorcha called from the kitchen doorway. "When did you first realize there was something there?"

Everyone turned to me, and my heart pounded in my ears. I'd spent the afternoon worried about this very question, but in the moment, I couldn't think of a single lie.

So instead, I told the truth.

"I'd always been aware of him," I admitted, staring into my second glass of wine rather than meet anyone's eyes. "There was something the first time I saw him. I didn't understand it. I just—felt it." I glanced at Calder, and found his eyes on mine.

"But then when we were decorating for the wedding—"

"Your magic recognized him," Sorcha said, slipping into the seat across from us. She looked like she was trying not to grin.

"Yes," I said softly. "It was reaching for him, and he was reaching back."

Calder's hand tightened around mine, and when I looked up at him, there was an expression on his face I couldn't read.

"That's when I knew this wasn't just in my head," I said. "And then when I woke up in my bed the day after the wedding, he was there. He'd carried me home the night before, checked the wards for me, and made sure the village was safe, even though he barely knew me. Who does that?"

The room was quiet for a moment. I'd meant to stick to simple facts, to the story we were crafting, but somehow I'd ended up saying more than I meant to about how he affected me.

But Sorcha simply sighed, a dreamy sound that broke the silence. "That's so romantic," she said, as she put her elbows on the table, cradling her head in her hands. "The magic knowing before you did. It's like the stories my grandmother used to tell about fated pairs."

I laughed before I realized she wasn't teasing. Fated pairs? Was that what she thought this was?

Conor, grinning broadly, raised his glass in a toast. "To magic knowing what we need before we do. And to two of my favorite people finally finding each other."

The conversation, thankfully, drifted to lighter topics—village gossip, their honeymoon trip to the southern valley, plans for the upcoming harvest festival. I relaxed into the familiar company of friends, while the wine warmed my blood and loosened my tongue. Calder kept his hand on my knee under the table, a touch that looked innocent enough, and felt anything but.

By my third glass of wine, I sat sideways in my chair, leaned into his warmth and the deep rumble of his laugh when Conor told a story about a mishap with a fishing net. The flickering candlelight caught the angles of his face, shadows accentuating the sharp cut of his jaw, the curve of his mouth.

"More wine?" Conor asked, already refilling my glass before I could answer.

"Careful," Calder murmured, his breath warm against my ear. "You're two ahead of me."

"Are you keeping count?" I whispered back, irritated that he was babysitting me, but strangely pleased to know I had his attention.

"Maybe I just want to make sure you'll be steady enough to walk home," he replied, the corner of his mouth lifting in that almost-smile.

"And if I'm not?" I wondered what it would be like to have him carry me again—this time without the inconvenience of being unconscious.

"Then I guess I've had two practice runs," he squeezed my knee before retreating.

I missed his touch immediately, which bothered me enough that I focused all my attention on my berry tart for the next several minutes.

When Sorcha and Conor stepped into the kitchen to fetch more wine, Calder leaned in close, his voice pitched low. "You're brilliant, you know that?" he murmured. "They believe every word."

I turned to respond and found his face much closer than I'd expected, our noses nearly touching. "You think so?" I breathed, unable to look away from the gold flecks in his irises.

"Absolutely," he said, grinning. "You're terrifying."

I blinked, then smiled.

"Thank you," I said, and meant it.

Sorcha and Conor returned with another bottle. I reluctantly leaned away from Calder.

"Oh, don't let us interrupt," Sorcha said with a grin, noticing our proximity.

"We were just talking," I said, the words coming out more defensively than I'd intended.

Conor snorted.

"Hush, you," Sorcha chided, swatting at him with a tea towel before turning to us with suspiciously innocent eyes. "So. Who's moving in with who?"

I choked on my last bite of tart.

"Sorcha!" I said, barely coughing out her name.

"What?" she said innocently, topping off my glass. "It's perfectly reasonable to assume you'd be living together."

"Before the binding ceremony?" Conor asked.

"We did!" Sorcha argued.

"We haven't really talked about it," I said, butting in. Which was technically true. "Not yet."

"Not yet," Sorcha repeated, eyes narrowing with delight.

"We're figuring it out," Calder, mercifully, jumped in. "I'm working on earning the privilege."

Everyone laughed, but I didn't. It was a joke, something to lighten the mood, I knew that.

If I thought I'd been blushing before, now my entire body felt like it was on fire. The gentle pressure of his fingers against my leg sent sparks dancing along my thigh.

"A male who respects boundaries," Conor nodded approvingly.

"And one who knows good things are worth waiting for," Calder added, winking.

"Speaking of waiting," Sorcha said, stretching luxuriously, "I've held off on the sordid details of our honeymoon long enough. Let me tell you about this little beach we found..."

I wasn't sure if he was conscious of it or if it was just something to do with his hands, but Calder's thumb began tracing idle circles on my knee, and I found myself melting under his touch.

The wine and the candlelight and the laughter—it was all too easy to forget that this wasn't how things really were.

By the time Sorcha finished her third honeymoon story, the

candles had burned low, and my head was pleasantly fuzzy from the wine. Calder's arm had somehow found its way around the back of my chair, his fingers occasionally brushing my shoulder.

"We should probably go," I said reluctantly, when a lull in the conversation allowed. "It's getting late."

"Already?" Sorcha pouted, though her eyes were heavy-lidded with wine and the lateness of the hour. "But we were just getting to the good parts."

"Some other time," I promised, rising from my chair and immediately swaying on my feet. Perhaps those last few glasses had been a mistake.

Calder was there, his arm sliding around my waist to steady me. The familiar pulse of our magic meeting crawled down my spine.

"I've got you," he murmured, close enough that I could feel his breath against my temple.

I should have pulled away, should have insisted I was fine, but the solid strength of him felt too good to give up. So I let myself lean into him, just a little.

"This was wonderful," I said to Sorcha and Conor as we stood at their door, genuinely grateful for the evening.

"We should do it again soon," Conor suggested, his arm wrapped around Sorcha's waist. "Maybe at your place next time, Meira?"

"Or mine," Calder offered. "Once I finish that table it'll be more suitable for entertaining."

Sorcha hugged me tightly, whispering in my ear, "I haven't seen you this happy in years."

She should have just punched me in the gut. I didn't know if I could respond, so I simply hugged her back before we said our final goodnights.

The night air was sobering. I shivered, missing Calder's

warmth immediately when he released me to close the door behind us.

But as soon as we started walking, his arm returned to my waist, guiding me through the darkened village streets. I told myself it was because I was unsteady from the wine, but that didn't stop me from leaning into him.

"That went well," he said after a while, his deep voice rumbling through me where our sides pressed together. "I think they believe us."

"Mmm," I agreed, too caught up in the sensation of his fingers splayed against my ribs to form coherent thoughts.

We reached my cottage far too quickly. I turned to face him at the door, reluctant to end the evening.

"Thank you," I said, looking up at him in the moonlight. "For tonight. For all of it."

"I enjoyed myself," he replied, and there was a softness in his voice I hadn't heard before. "Our friends are good people."

"They are," I agreed. Then, feeling bold from the wine and the lingering magic of the evening, I added, "Would you like to come in? For tea, or..."

He didn't answer, but his eyes dropped to my lips.

For a heartbeat, I thought he might accept, might follow me inside and—what? My mind raced with possibilities, each more dangerous than the last.

But he shook his head, his smile gentle but tinged with regret. "Not tonight," he said, his voice deeper than usual. "You've had a lot of wine, and I..." He trailed off, his eyes still fixed on my mouth. "I want to get some sleep before the ward work tomorrow."

It wasn't a rejection, not exactly. But it felt close enough to one anyway.

"Tomorrow, then?" I asked, trying my best to sound neutral. "The northern ward? I typically go before sunrise."

"I'll meet you there before sunrise," he promised. Then, with a deliberate slowness that gave me plenty of time to pull away, he leaned down.

I held my breath, his lips brushed the corner of my mouth, not quite a proper kiss but my body didn't know the difference. His hand came up to cup my face, his thumb tracing the line of my jaw.

"Goodnight, Meira," he murmured against my skin, his breath warm and wine-sweet.

"Goodnight," I whispered, frozen in place.

I watched as he walked away, the moonlight silvering his dark hair as he disappeared into the night. I stood, unmoved, long after he was gone.

Only when I was inside, the door firmly closed behind me, did I let myself feel it. My body was humming with awareness, with need, with the lingering effects of his proximity. Every place he'd touched me felt branded, alive in a way I'd never experienced before.

I sank onto my bed, still fully dressed, and stared unseeing at the ceiling. The truth I'd been running from all evening caught up with me at last, impossible to ignore in the solitude of my room:

I wanted him. Not for the sake of the wards, not for the lie I'd told the Council, but for myself. And that was terrifying.

12

—————

I slept in the dress.

Last night I stood in front of the mirror, staring at the buttons that ran down my back, and told myself I should undo them. That I should take it off gently, fold it neatly, and drape it over the chair the way I always did with the things I wanted to keep nice.

But I couldn't move. I just stood there, staring at my own reflection, afraid that getting out of the dress would break whatever spell had settled over the night.

If I took it off, would I still feel the exact spot where Calder's hand had held my waist? Would I still feel where his lips pressed next to mine?

I didn't want to risk it.

So I crawled into bed with the buttons still fastened, my hair still done, and let myself pretend it hadn't ended.

The dress still smelled like him, cedar and woodsmoke.

Sleep should have come easy, but my mind wouldn't stop looping through every look, every word, and every brush of his hand.

I laid there for the longest time, trying to memorize the

warmth of his hand on my knee. The way his thumb had moved, barely, like he wasn't sure if he was allowed to want more.

I slept eventually, and woke before dawn, but knew I wouldn't fall back asleep.

I brewed the last of Aoife's bitter tea, drowned it in honey, and dragged my thickest sweater over the top of last night's dress. As if something soft could soothe the part of me that still felt undone. It hung past my hips, the sleeves were too long, and the neckline slouched off one shoulder, but it felt right.

The sky outside was still black, the mist thick over the grass, and I could see every breath, but I needed air.

I stepped out into the cold morning and sank onto the stone steps. With the mug of tea cradled in both hands, I let the warmth seep into my fingers and tried not to think about Calder. Which, of course, meant I could think of nothing else.

Then I heard footsteps, boots on stone.

Someone coming up the path from the village square. I never saw villagers out this way early in the morning.

As the figure stepped through the fog, it was broad and tall and achingly familiar.

"Calder," I hissed, my heart still slamming against my ribs. "Gods. You scared the shit out of me."

He raised both hands in surrender, a small white paper box clutched in one. "I didn't mean to scare you, I had no idea you'd be awake."

His hair was still damp, curling at the ends. His shirt half-unbuttoned at the collar, cloak hanging off his shoulder like he'd only remembered to throw it on as he was already out the door.

"Did you come from the square?" I asked. "There's nothing even open right now."

"Fern's husband bakes early on fishing days," he said, stepping onto the porch and offering me the box. "I caught him just as the first tray came out."

I opened the box slowly, there were two warm pastries inside. "You got up before sunrise to bring me a cinnamon bun?"

The sugar and cinnamon hit my nose and it was everything I could not to groan. Instead, I blinked too fast, and swallowed the ache in my throat. I lifted one out of the box and took a bite, and this time I couldn't stop the sound I made.

"I figured if I showed up early, I shouldn't do so empty-handed."

"Smart male."

Calder grinned until his gaze caught on something behind me, toward the door. He crouched beside it, fingers brushing a narrow split in the frame.

"There's a crack here."

I shrugged. "It's an old house."

"Hmm," was all he offered in response.

I shifted to the side, leaving space beside me in case he wanted to sit. He did.

He sat with a soft groan, arms braced behind him, legs stretching long. When he shifted, his knee brushed mine. The contact was casual, probably unintentional, but it shot through me all the same.

"Are you..." he cleared his throat, suddenly sheepish. "Is that the same dress you wore last night?"

"Couldn't get it off," I muttered around a bite.

His mouth twitched. He tried to hold it back, but the grin slipped through. "Do you need help, Meira?"

I looked at him out of the corner of my eye, and dared him to keep going.

"Or were you planning to wear it all day?" he added.

"I was," I said flatly, rising. "But since you're offering—yes, Calder, I need your help. Please help me unbutton my dress."

I wasn't sure what possessed me, but the way his eyes widened made it impossible to stop. I handed him the rest of the cinnamon bun, pulled off the sweater, and turned my back to him.

The cold slipped across my skin through the dress's fabric. I gathered my hair over one shoulder, exposing the line of tiny buttons that marched down my spine.

"Are you going to help me?" I teased, over my shoulder.

He exhaled hard and stood. I didn't move, even when I could feel the warmth of his breath on the nape of my neck.

His fingers fumbled the top button. "Why are these so small?" he grumbled.

I smiled, despite myself. "I can get the top three, it's the middle ones I can't reach."

I undid them slowly, feeling his gaze as much as his presence. Then I stopped and let him take over.

His calloused fingers dipped just inside the parted fabric as he fought with the next clasp. His hands were warmer than I expected. After several moments, one of the buttons slipped free. Then another.

He unfastened several more, far more than he needed to, and each time his callused fingertips grazed my spine, I had to resist the urge to lean into him. Every brush of his fingers down my spine left a trail of heat in their wake. When he reached the small of my back, his hand stilled.

I turned slightly, just enough to glance back. "That's enough," I whispered.

He nodded, but didn't step back.

"Unless," I added softly, opening the door, "you'd like to finish helping me in here."

Calder looked at the open door, then at me, the want clear in his eyes. He handed me the cinnamon bun with a smile that didn't reach his mouth. "Another time."

Then he stepped back, and let me go.

I changed quickly, pulled on a loose tunic with leggings, and swept my hair half up, letting the rest fall around my shoulders.

When I came back, Calder was waiting inside the door, holding it open for me. We didn't speak as I laced up my boots. But I could still feel his fingers, and goosebumps trailed the full length of my back.

We walked the cobblestone path in silence until it gave way to the packed dirt that led toward the forest.

"I hope it's okay to take the long way," I said. "I didn't ask if you were busy today."

"Fine by me," he replied.

By the time we reached the northern stone, sunlight had broken over the mountains. Dew clung to the meadow, and birds chattered in the trees. Somewhere near the river, a fox yipped playfully.

The northern stone stood in the dip of the meadow, the dew across its face shimmered in the morning light. The power between stones hummed lightly, it had become such a comforting sound.

Calder shifted his weight as we approached, his boots sinking slightly into the softened earth. He moved instinctively toward the southern flank of the stone where the current was typically thinnest.

I drifted to the opposite side, tracing my fingertips lightly over a patch of moss curling up the base. The air smelled like damp bark, earthy and old. I sank to my knees beside the anchor point, brushing dew from the edge of the stone.

A flicker of tension passed just above the ground beneath my palm. It wasn't a tear yet, just a fraying edge. At the same time, Calder and I both stilled.

I looked up, he was already studying the stone, eyes narrowed slightly, his head tilted like he was listening for something. I couldn't hear anything out of the ordinary, but we both felt it.

Without a word, I reached for the fraying thread of power. My own magic slid from my palm in a slow, uneven line, sluggish but obedient. A single strand of gold stretches towards the frayed ward line, pulsing faintly.

Across from me, Calder adjusted his stance. Slowly, he lowered himself into the grass next to me, and extended his hand toward the thread. He didn't touch it, just moved close enough to change the shape of the air.

Just as my own magic wavered, his answered the call. The same familiar pressure I'd come to recognize moved in closer. He didn't try to take over, he just curled his own power around the edges of mine, anchoring it without force.

I tracked the way his jaw flexed when the thread dipped. The way he shifted his weight as we worked, knees spread, boots braced against the soft earth like he'd done this a thousand times. One hand hovered steady above the current, the other loosely curled in his lap.

He let me lead the weaving of the wards, but I could feel him there, matching my rhythm, keeping pace. Every time I started to slip, his presence intuitively steadied me.

Mending the wards had never been this smooth, with Calder or on my own. When the final thread was in place, a soft pulse ran through the stone as the power anchored itself. Done.

I sat back on my heels, trying not to shiver as the warmth faded from my fingertips. Calder lowered his hand, resting it on his knee and finally looked at me.

We watched each other for a beat too long.

"Do you have time this morning?" he asked, voice quiet.

I nodded.

"I have something to show you."

I followed him away from the wardstones, in the opposite

direction of the village, and with each step, the familiar hum of protective magic grew fainter.

"Where are we going?" I asked, trying to keep the edge out of my voice.

"Somewhere I found a few weeks ago." Calder glanced back at me.

We walked for nearly half an hour, the forest growing wilder around us. I'd never walked this far beyond the boundary. There were no more neat paths to follow, just ancient trees and undergrowth that crunched under my boots.

Finally, he led me through a break in the trees and the clearing beyond was so beautiful, I understood why the forest had hidden it.

A waterfall spilled down black rock into a small pool so clear I could see smooth stones on the bottom. Purple lupines grew wild along the banks. The sound of water on stone echoed off the surrounding cliffs.

Everything felt untouched, like no one had ever stood here before us.

"How did you find this?" I whispered.

"I found it by accident last week." His voice was closer than I expected. When I turned, his eyes stayed on mine. "Spent the whole walk back thinking about showing it to you."

My fingers brushed the edge of my tunic where it had twisted near my hip.

Calder's gaze dropped to my mouth. That was all it took.

I closed the space between us, and his hand rose to cup my cheek, thumb grazing my jaw like he needed to memorize it. His other hand settled at my waist, anchoring me to him.

And then he kissed me.

He kissed me like he'd made peace with the consequences. Like he knew this could ruin everything and chose me anyway.

I leaned into him, my fingers curled in the open edge of his shirt. I pulled him closer, and he made a low sound in his throat that sent heat racing through me. His mouth moved against mine with a hunger that made my knees weak, and I matched it without hesitation.

He slid a hand into my hair and tilted my head back, and when his lips found my neck, I couldn't stop the sound that escaped me. He kissed along my throat, each touch making me arch closer to him, until I was pressed against him completely.

When he finally pulled back to look at me, we were both breathing hard.

His thumb brushed my lip, and something deep in my chest gave way, like the first crack in a dam holding back everything I hadn't let myself feel, everything I hadn't let myself want.

Standing there in his arms, with the sound of water falling over stone and his heart beating against my chest, it would be easy to fall in love with Calder.

Maybe I already was.

13

———

I couldn't focus on a damned thing in my shop. At least, none of the orders I should have been working on.

I enchanted a few of Brenna's bar towels to clean spills on their own—a small, quick charm that didn't take my mind off Calder for long. So I did the whole stack. And the backups. And a few cloths that weren't even hers.

She didn't ask, but I needed something to fix, so I fixed what I could. Then I charmed the brooms to sweep floors that didn't need it and rearranged the same three vials four times, just to feel like something in my life was still in my control.

"Oh good, you're here." Sorcha burst through the door with the confidence of a woman who'd known me since we were three—and had never once respected a boundary.

"I brought pastries," she announced, slapping a paper-wrapped bundle onto the counter. "And my notes."

"For what?" I asked, though I had a good idea.

Sorcha gave me a look. The one she saved for idiots. "The handfasting, Meira. We are not going to let Elder Muriel bind you two in that dusty old chamber like it's a tax hearing. You're going to have a proper ceremony with flowers."

My stomach turned. "We don't even have a date."

"Which is why we're choosing one now." She began unfurling a roll of parchment like it was a battle map. "It takes time to enchant all those floating lights, especially if you want them to sparkle the way mine did. You want them to sparkle, don't you?"

Before I could escape, a knock hit the doorframe. Brenna stood there, hair pinned haphazardly, eyes sharp.

"Am I late?"

"You're perfect," Sorcha said, already motioning her in. "Meira was just agreeing to let us take over her evening."

"I brought cider," Brenna said, holding up the jug like a peace offering. "And gossip. Also, Calder's down at the tavern helping Willem with those long benches the Murphy boys cracked in their latest brawl. We should stop by."

"I'm not interrupting his work just so we can—"

"You're already blushing," Brenna said as she breezed past me.

"I am not."

"You are," Sorcha added. "Your ears are red as roses."

I was not blushing, I was unraveling, but I let them drag me anyway.

THE TAVERN WAS TOO WARM, too full, and too loud.

Lantern-light shimmered on the walls, catching in the glass of the half-empty mugs littering every table.The tavern roared with noise. Conversations tangled together, chairs ground against stone, cutlery rang against plates like scattered bells.

Calder was crouched low near the hearth, sleeves rolled, forearms dusted with wood shavings, fitting a carved support beam beneath a table.

He shifted his weight as we entered, pressing his palm flat

against the wood as he drove the new brace into place. He was focused, and completely unaware he had all of my attention.

One hand braced the bench, while the other tested the joinery, his knuckles flecked with oil. His shirt clung slightly to his back where the fire's heat had sunk in.

Then Brenna, from behind the bar, tossed a towel straight at his face.

Without even getting up from his crouched position, Calder reached up and caught it with one hand and slung it over his shoulder with the kind of ease that only came from always knowing what was happening around him.

Someone whistled. Someone else said something about "forest fae reflexes," and the table next to him laughed.

He smiled, barely, and looked up.

His eyes found mine in an instant, across the entire tavern, like he'd just known I was there. I felt like we were the only two people in the room.

I turned away first.

"Willem said to take the table by the window," Brenna said, steering us. "I'll bring plates."

The bench was warm when I sat, the grain smooth from Calder's hands.

Sorcha settled beside me, parchment already unrolling. "We have a lot to cover. Flowers. Music. Ceremony order."

"Sorcha no, nothing like that. This is just a formality."

She ignored me entirely, "Are you having a veil? You should have a veil."

"I'm not—"

"Fine, no veil. But you're wearing a wedding dress," she said, and she sounded exasperated. "I'm not budging on that."

My magic buzzed under my skin, restless and useless. I couldn't stop watching him. I hadn't stopped thinking about him for days since that kiss.

"Stop staring," Brenna muttered as she passed behind me.

"I'm not—"

"You are."

I sipped my cider and shut my mouth.

The door opened, and more villagers came in, but I barely noticed, because Calder crossed the room. He moved in the same way he always did. He moved through every room like he belonged, and the whole tavern shifted to make space for him.

Even under Sorcha's death stare, he didn't balk. Just walked straight over to our table and stopped at my side.

"Have any space for me?" he asked, voice low.

"No," Sorcha said brightly, in a mocking tone that someone might reserve for their siblings, "but we'll make room anyway."

Sorcha got up and went to the other side of the table so Calder could sit beside me. He left space so that we weren't even close enough to brush sleeves, but the heat of him reached me through the air anyway.

His scent hit me a second later. Cedar and woodsmoke, and a hint of rosemary from the roast he must've helped carry to the kitchen. I suddenly couldn't remember how to sit without being aware of every line of my body.

Brenna brought food. She returned with plates filled with roast, greens, and fresh bread. The smell alone made my stomach clench with hunger. Brenna slid onto the bench beside Sorcha. Beside me, Calder ate with the same steady rhythm he did everything else.

Across the table, Sorcha was still talking about veils and ribbons and ceremonial wine, but I couldn't follow a word.

Because Calder's thigh brushed mine under the table, just barely. If tension could catch, the touch would have started a fire. I didn't move, and he didn't either. I wouldn't have budged even if I *had* caught fire.

"Too much?" he murmured, low and lazy. He knew it absolutely was.

I couldn't answer. I was too busy pretending to breathe.

His hand rested on the bench between us, fingers drumming lightly, slowly, in a rhythm that matched my heartbeat far too well.

"You're staring again," Brenna said with her fork pointed at me.

"I am not."

"You are." She pointed at Calder. "And so is he."

Calder didn't deny it.

Later, after the plates had been cleared and the heat from the hearth had sunk deep into my skin. The tavern began to blur at the edges, the room grew even louder, until I was blanketed under a layer layer of noise, and still, I felt the weight of Calder beside me.

I didn't see him as he leaned in—only that suddenly his mouth was near my ear, and the world hushed around the sound of his voice.

"Would you like to step outside?" he asked, quietly enough that no one else heard.

I turned to him, to that impossible closeness, and nodded.

"Yes," I said, too quickly.

I set my cup down with more force than necessary and stood. The bench scraped the floor behind me, the sound sharp enough to turn a few heads. I saw Sorcha and Brenna looking at me out of the corner of my eye, but I didn't look back. Just walked, heart hammering, skin flushed, magic humming low and reckless beneath the surface.

He followed without a word.

The hallway off the main room was narrow and dim, cooler where the warmth of the firelight no longer reached. The floors creaked, the old wood shifting under our feet, not caring how hard I was trying to be quiet. Lantern light flickered near the back door, and cast our shadows along the walls.

I stopped just short of the door. He stood close enough that I could feel the shape of him behind me.

He reached toward the door, probably assuming I was waiting for him to open it for me, but I smacked his hand away.

"What the—"

"I thought we were meant to be pretending to be together," I hissed.

"We are," he frowned. "Meant to be."

"Then why does it feel like this?"

His expression didn't change, but something in his stance did. A month ago I might not have noticed, but I was too in tune with him now.

"You *ravaged* me the other day," I said, crossing my arms.

His jaw tensed slightly. "You ravaged me back."

I stepped closer, close enough to feel the warmth radiating off his skin, close enough to see how tightly he was wound beneath that careful calm. "Are you still pretending, Calder?"

He looked at my mouth, then my eyes. He didn't say a word.

The want, the *need* to feel his lips on me was boiling over, tingling all across my skin. He still hadn't answered me, so I asked again—differently this time. "Are we still pretending?"

He exhaled like it hurt. "I don't know."

This time, I didn't wait. I couldn't take it anymore.

I lunged at him, and when our bodies collided, I pressed my hands to his chest and fisted his shirt in one hand, and reached for his neck with the other. It didn't take much to pull him to me, he was already meeting me halfway. I kissed him like I'd been holding my own breath all day, and only he could give me the air I so desperately needed.

A week ago I would have been afraid, would have second guessed this. But I knew in my bones that if I didn't take what I wanted right now, I might never let myself want it again.

He caught me in an instant, hands at my waist, pulling me flush against him with a sound low in his throat. The kiss deepened fast—too fast—and I didn't care.

Gods, I didn't care.

His mouth was desperate and sure and everything I hadn't let myself feel. He tasted like cider and cinnamon and I wanted to drink every bit of him in. His hand slid to the small of my back, mine curled into the collar of his shirt.

A door closed down the hall, and it was just enough that we finally broke apart, but neither of us stepped back. No one appeared, we were still alone.

I was still breathing hard, skin flushed and aching, the echo of his mouth on mine ringing through every nerve. His hands were still at my waist. Mine were tangled in his hair.

He leaned in again—but not for another kiss. This time, his lips brushed the curve of my jaw, then lower, tracing the line of my neck with slow, deliberate softness. My breath caught.

"This is a bad idea," I whispered, but the words barely made it out.

His mouth found the hollow beneath my ear, and his lips brushed my skin. "Then tell me to stop."

I didn't. I should have, I knew that, but I couldn't. My heart was pounding too loud in my ears, my whole body felt tight.

My fingers loosened in his hair, and I let my hands slide down the back of his neck, anchoring myself like letting go wasn't an option.

"Maybe I should go," I said, even though it came out thin and unconvincing.

He didn't lift his head, just let the words hang between us.

"If you go back and say goodbye to the girls," he murmured into my hair, voice rough against my skin, "I'll walk you home."

I closed my eyes. I wasn't ready to move. I didn't trust what I'd do if I did.

"And if I don't want to go home?" The question came out in a breathy whisper.

His breath caught at that, and he pulled back just enough to look into my eyes. He held my gaze like he could see exactly what I was afraid to say. "Then I'll follow you anywhere."

14

____

We walked to the cottage in complete silence, neither of us willing to shatter the moment. Inside, I walked halfway into the living room before turning around and watching him shut the door behind his back.

I met him halfway.

I slid my hands up his chest, under his shirt this time, palms skimming over his warm skin.

He caught my face between his hands and held me there. Not to stop me, just to be with me.

"I don't know what we're doing," I said. "But I know I want it."

His eyes searched mine.

"I do too," he said. "Fuck, Meira. Of course I do."

He bent his head towards me, and let me close that last inch between us.

When our mouths met this time, there was no hesitation. This was us finally reaching for what we'd been denying ourselves.

His eyes darkened, and for a moment he didn't move—just

stared at me like he was trying to etch every part of me into memory.

Then he kissed me again, slower and deeper this time. There had never been a moment we didn't want this.

When his hands slipped beneath my shirt and found bare skin, every nerve sang in recognition. Nothing about him was foreign. His hands on me felt like remembering. My body had always known the shape of his palms, the weight of his touch.

We moved together, toward the bedroom. A slow backward shuffle of kisses and laughter and tangled breath, as my fingers tugged at the laces of his shirt and he slid further under mine like he couldn't decide if he wanted to remove the barrier or just learn me by touch.

My knees hit the edge of the bed and I let myself fall back, legs still hanging over the side, breathing hard, smiling like a fool.

Calder paused, standing over me in the low light, his shirt undone, chest rising and falling like he was working just as hard to stay grounded.

Then he froze.

"I brought something," he said, suddenly awkward. "In case this happened. It's a tincture from Aoife, I mean. For, ah—"

"Contraception?" I offered, breathless and grinning.

He nodded once. "She said she could see right through us, and I'd better be prepared."

My laugh was full and loud, the tension breaking across my ribs in a wave.

"Smart woman," I said.

"She really is."

"Do I need to drink it?"

"No," he said. "It's mine. I took it earlier. Just in case."

I blinked, that familiar warmth blooming in the center of my chest.

"You thought we might..."

"No," he said quickly. "Not tonight, necessarily. I just—I hoped we would eventually. And I didn't want anything to make you pause, if you chose to want this."

My heart didn't just ache, it gave way entirely.

I sat up slowly, and reached for him.

"I want this," I said again. "All of it. All of you."

He bent to kiss me again. And this time when I pulled his shirt off completely and let my fingers wander lower, he didn't stop me.

He leaned over me as I lay back, slow and careful, like he didn't want to startle everything taking shape between us. The bed dipped beneath his weight, and the moment he settled above me, propped on one arm and the other skimming up my thigh, I felt my whole body sigh into him.

He traced a path down my throat with his mouth, lingering at the hollow where my pulse hammered. When I arched against him, he groaned low in his chest—a sound that went straight through me.

I tugged my shirt over my head and tossed it aside while he watched. He went still, gaze traveling over me with an intensity that should have made me self-conscious. Instead, I felt powerful under his stare.

"Meira," he said, my name rough on his tongue.

"I want to feel you," I whispered.

Calder's breath hitched. He bowed his head, and when he looked up again, the restraint was gone—replaced by something raw, dark, and hungry.

Then he kissed me like he didn't care what came next.

My hands moved over his bare chest, down his back, across the wide span of his shoulders. I wanted to touch every part of him, to know what he felt like pressed against me, skin to skin, breath to breath.

When he reached for my waistband, he paused.

"Can I?" he asked, voice barely a breath.

"Yes." I cupped the back of his neck. "Please."

The way his eyes closed when I said that, like the word please undid him.

He undressed me with reverence, this wasn't just sex but the act of worshipping at long-last. And when I finally lay bare beneath him, completely exposed, I felt adored.

When he stood to undress, I sat up to watch. I wanted to see him, all of him. He was beautiful, strong in the quiet way that came from years of work, marked with scars that told stories I wanted to learn. When I reached out, he didn't pull away, but let me trace the largest one near his ribs.

I grabbed his waistband and pulled, hands fumbling at the laces, too desperate now to be elegant. He caught my wrists gently, not to stop me, but to still me.

"Are you sure?"

"Yes," I said, already breathless. "I'm so sure."

A flicker of relief crossed his face. He'd needed to hear it one more time, just to know I wasn't swept up in the moment. That I was choosing him with a clear head, a wild heart.

Then he let go, and I pulled his pants off of him, my knuckles brushing the heat of him beneath.

He was already hard, straining towards me. When I wrapped my fingers around him—slow, sure—he cursed under his breath, head dropping, hips moving forward.

"Meira..."

I stroked him once, twice, just to watch him come undone for me.

He reached for me then. Pushed me back onto the bed, his hands framing my hips, mouth crashing into mine again with a hunger that had finally tipped past restraint. He climbed over me, weight pressing me into the mattress, and every inch of skin on skin was a fuse lit straight down my spine.

"I can't take it slow," he said into my mouth. "Not this time."

"Then don't."

"I wanted to—I planned to—but gods, I can't—"

"Then don't," I said again, teeth grazing his jaw. "Next time. Go slow next time. Kill me with it later. Just—Calder—now."

He lined himself up, one hand braced on my thigh, the other cradling the back of my head, and pushed in with one long, desperate thrust.

I gasped, hips lifted to meet him.

He didn't stop. Didn't pause. Just buried himself deeper inside me until there was nothing between us.

He began to move, hard and fast and deep.

I wrapped my legs around his hips and held on.

Every thrust, every drag of him over that perfect, devastating place inside pulled a moan from me. I begged without words.

He drove into me harder.

"I'm going to come," I gasped. "I can't—Calder—"

"Let go," he said. "I've got you."

So I did.

I came hard, full-body, legs shaking beneath him as pleasure unraveled me from the inside out. Magic sparked beneath my skin, wild and bright and barely contained, like even it didn't know what to do with what I was feeling.

I clenched around him, and he groaned out my name and thrust deep once, twice, then spilled inside me with a broken sound, head buried in the crook of my neck, body shaking.

He stayed inside me, breathing hard. One hand tangled in my hair, the other pressed to my hip like he couldn't stand the thought of not touching me.

We were a tangle of sweat and breath and barely satiated need. I felt entirely wrecked and remade. My lips were swollen. I didn't care. I had never, in my life, felt so good.

So wanted.

He lifted his head eventually, kissed my cheek, my jaw, the hollow of my throat. He didn't speak. Neither did I.

Words felt too small for what had just formed between us.

Instead, I wrapped my arms around him, and pulled him down until his full weight covered me. He groaned, but didn't resist. Just pressed his forehead to mine and closed his eyes.

"Next time," he said softly, "we go slow."

I nodded. "So slow it kills us."

He grinned. His smile was soft, eyes dazed. He was beautiful. "You're going to kill me either way."

15

The first thing I felt was his hand at my waist, fingers tracing lazy circles against my skin like he'd been awake for a while, just touching me.

The second thing I felt was his mouth pressing soft kisses to my shoulder.

"Good morning," he murmured against my neck, voice rough with sleep.

I smiled before I even opened my eyes. "How long have you been awake?"

"Long enough to watch you sleep." His arm tightened around me, pulling me closer. "You make this little sound when you dream."

"I do not."

"You do." He nipped at my earlobe. "It's adorable."

He kissed the top of my shoulder, thumb sweeping lazy circles against my hip.

"What are you thinking about?" he asked.

I debated saying something poetic. The way his hands still felt on my skin. The way my heart was beating like it belonged to him now.

"We forgot to pay our tab."

He froze, then groaned into my neck. "Fuck."

I laughed so hard I shook the bed. "Brenna's going to make us scrub floors for a week."

"Worth it," he muttered as he kissed behind my ear. "But gods, we are never going to live that down."

I turned in his arms, finally opening my eyes to find him already looking at me. His hair was a mess, stubble dark along his jaw, and he looked absolutely devastating in the morning light.

"Hi," I whispered.

"Hi yourself." He cupped my face, thumb brushing my cheek. "How are you feeling?"

"Like I want to do that again."

His grin was pure sin. "Which part?"

"All of it." I stretched against him, enjoying the way his eyes darkened. "But maybe we should eat first. I'm starving."

"Good idea." He didn't move. Just kept looking at me like I was something miraculous. "Gods, you're beautiful."

I felt myself blush. "You're not so bad yourself."

"Just not so bad?" He raised an eyebrow, rolling until I was pinned beneath him. "Clearly I need to work harder to impress you."

"Calder—"

He silenced me with a kiss, slow and thorough. His hands roamed over me like he was relearning every curve, every sensitive spot he'd discovered last night. When he found the place where my neck met my shoulder and bit down gently, I arched against him with a gasp.

"There's my girl," he murmured.

My girl. The words sent heat spiraling through me.

"Is that what I am?" I asked breathlessly.

He pulled back to look at me, expression suddenly serious. "If you want to be."

"Yes," I said without hesitation. "Yes, I want to be yours."

Something fierce and possessive flashed in his eyes. "Good. Because I'm not letting you go."

He kissed me again, hungrier this time, and I felt that familiar fire building between us. His hand slipped between my thighs, finding me already wet for him.

"Already?" he asked, pleased.

"Already," I breathed, then gasped as his fingers found exactly the right spot. "Calder—"

"Shh," he whispered against my mouth. "Let me take care of you."

And he did. Slowly, thoroughly, until I was writhing beneath him. When I finally came apart around his fingers, he swallowed my cries with his mouth.

"Beautiful," he breathed, watching my face as I came down. "Absolutely beautiful."

I reached for him, and found him hard and ready. "My turn."

But when I tried to return the favor, he caught my wrists. "Later. Right now I just want to be inside you."

He entered me slowly this time, both of us sighing at the connection. It felt different than last night, like we had all the time in the world to learn each other.

The rhythm we found was gentle but building slowly until we were both trembling with need. When I came, it was with his name on my lips and his eyes locked on mine. He followed moments later, burying his face in my neck as he shuddered against me.

We lay tangled together afterward, catching our breath. I traced patterns on his chest while he played with my hair.

"I could get used to this," I said softly.

"You'd better." His arm tightened around me. "Because I'm planning on keeping you in this bed for the foreseeable future."

I laughed. "The wards—"

"Can wait." He tilted my chin up. "One morning. Give me one morning where you're just mine and the rest of the world doesn't exist."

Looking into his eyes, I couldn't bring myself to argue. "One morning."

"Good." He rolled out of bed, gloriously naked and completely unbothered. "Now, you mentioned something about being hungry."

I watched him pad to the basin, marveling at the easy way he moved in my space, like he belonged here. Like this was already home for both of us.

"Tea?" I asked, wrapping the sheet around myself.

"Please." He caught me around the waist as I passed, spinning me into his arms. "But first—"

Another kiss, deeper this time. I melted into him, marveling at how natural it felt to be with him, how right.

"You taste like honey," he murmured against my mouth.

"That's my magic you're tasting."

"I like it." His hands roamed down my back.

Making tea took twice as long as usual because he couldn't seem to stop touching me. Fingers trailing down my arm as I measured leaves. A kiss to my temple while we waited for the water to boil. His arms around me from behind, chin resting on my shoulder.

"This is dangerous," I said as he nuzzled my neck.

"What is?"

"This. You. The way you make me feel like nothing else matters."

"Maybe nothing else does," he said simply.

I leaned back against his chest, feeling more content than I had in years.

"I loved waking up next to you."

I turned in his arms, heart hammering.

"Does that mean I get to have more mornings like this?" I asked quietly.

"If you'll have me." His thumb traced my cheek. "I meant what I said last night, Meira. I want this. I want you. Not just for one night."

Relief flooded through me so suddenly I felt dizzy. "Good. Because I want this too. All of it."

His smile was brilliant. "Yeah?"

"Yeah." I grinned back. "Probably more than I should."

We stood grinning at each other like fools until the whistle demanded attention.

"Tea," I said breathlessly.

"Tea," he agreed, but neither of us moved.

Even then, he kept his hands on me as I poured the water, as if he couldn't bear to break contact.

"We should probably get dressed eventually," I said after we ate, moving to pour more tea.

"Should we?" He appeared behind me, his mouth found that spot behind my ear. "I like you like this."

"The wards—"

"Will be there this afternoon." He took the cups from my hands, setting them on the table. "Won't they?"

Looking into his eyes, warm and wanting and completely focused on me, I decided they absolutely would.

"This afternoon," I agreed, already reaching for him.

He lifted me onto the counter, stepped between my legs, and kissed me like we had all the time in the world.

And maybe we did.

16

———

We did eventually make it out of the cottage, though neither of us was in any hurry. Every time I tried to braid my hair, Calder would kiss my neck and I'd lose track of what I was doing. Every time he reached for his boots, I'd find an excuse to touch him.

"We're going to be so late," I said, finally managing to get my own boots on.

"Worth it," he said, pulling me against him for one more kiss. He traced the line of my jaw with his thumb. "Though if you keep looking at me like that, we might not make it out of here at all."

I laughed, pushing him toward the door. "Out. Now. Before I change my mind."

The walk to the eastern wardstone should have taken twenty minutes. It took closer to an hour, because I couldn't stop stealing glances at the way Calder moved through the dappled sunlight, and he couldn't seem to pass a single tree without finding an excuse to press me against it.

By the time we reached the stone, the sun was fully up and

the morning mist was beginning to burn off. The wardstone stood ancient and imposing, its surface carved with protective runes that seemed to shift in the changing light.

"Ready?" I asked, settling my palm against the warm stone.

"Always," he said, taking up position beside me.

Our magic met like it always did—his steady and sure, mine wild and bright. But this time felt more intimate somehow. Every brush of his power against mine sent warmth spiraling through me, and I found myself stealing glances at him as we worked.

"Focus," he murmured, but his eyes were dancing with amusement.

"I am focused."

"On the wards, Meira. Not on me."

"I can multitask."

He laughed, the sound rumbling through our shared magic and making the stone hum with approval. The wards responded to our connection, threads of power weaving together more smoothly than they ever had before.

"It's never been this easy," I said, watching the magic flow between us.

"Maybe because we're not fighting it anymore," he said quietly.

I looked up at him, finding his gaze already on mine. The magic pulsed around us, warm and golden, binding us together in every way.

"Calder—"

A cry split the silence. Sharp keening, the sound of something in terrible pain.

I froze, my hand still pressed against the stone. "What was that?"

But he was already moving.

He took a few steps toward the sound, and his body went still as he listened, eyes darting around the meadow.

Another cry followed, louder this time—a thin, pained whimper that twisted in my stomach.

I followed close behind him, and in the tall grass we found the source of the cries. A small fox, no bigger than a house cat, lay trembling in dew-soaked wildflowers. Its front leg was caught in a metal trap, brutal and rusted, teeth clamped tight around its shoulder. Blood slicked the russet fur down to its paw. Its sides heaved too fast, too shallow.

"Oh gods," I whispered.

Calder lowered to his knees in the grass next to the fox. I bent down, to do what I didn't know, but he stuck his arm out, blocking me from getting any closer.

"Don't—just stay back a second," he demanded. "Let me."

His voice was different now, commanding in a way I'd never heard before, like instinct had taken over. Realizing how he'd sounded, he said as if in apology: "I just don't want you to get hurt."

I did as he asked without arguing and didn't move.

The fox let out a high-pitched yelp as Calder reached out his hand, flinching before he'd even touched the trap.

I watched as he looked from the animal to the mechanism itself. He stared at the trap for a moment, and a look of recognition fell over his face. His nostrils flared and he clenched his teeth. He was *angry.*

One hand hovered above the wound, he carefully pressed his palm a few inches from the fox's flank. It reminded me of how I'd watched him fix the bench before Sorcha's wedding. He slid his forearm into the fox's hip to stabilize it, and now with the use of both hands, he braced the metal jaws.

The fox bit him, hard.

It was so quick, I gasped, but Calder didn't even flinch. He just closed his fingers around the trap and forced it open.

The teeth released with a sharp click. He slipped the iron away, and the fox lay still. I thought it might take off, but it didn't even try to move. He lifted the fox in his arms, careful not to touch its injured leg. It whimpered, but didn't fight. Just curled into him, trembling.

I stood frozen, watching with my stomach clenched as Calder cradled the tiny animal. Blood streaked down the inside of his forearm, a mix of his and the fox's, still dripping from where it had bitten him when he'd braced to open the trap. He didn't seem to notice.

"What can I do?" I asked.

"I'll take her to Aoife," he said, voice quieter now but still tight. "She's mended worse." He moved protectively, like he was still expecting something to go wrong. Whatever instincts had risen in him hadn't died down.

"I'll walk you back," he added.

I stepped toward him.

He didn't back away, but his posture shifted. He angled his body just slightly, turning the fox out of reach, putting himself in between. It was protective without posturing, like he didn't want to risk it hurting me.

I stopped a breath away, close enough to see the strain in his shoulders, the blood still trailing down his arm.

I looked up, hoping to be able to read something, anything, in his expression. Hoping he'd tell me what he was thinking without making me ask.

Instead, he leaned in, and pressed his lips to mine like he couldn't keep himself from it. Just once. There was no heat this time, just a gentle affirmation. Forehead to mine, we took a slow breath together.

"Go," I whispered, not trusting my voice with much more. "Go to Aoife's. I'll meet you there."

He nodded, and without looking back, cut across the meadow back to the village.

I stayed where I was, letting the morning sun wash over me.

The warmth should have been comforting, but all I could think about was the gentle press of his lips. I had the strangest feeling he'd taken something of mine with him.

17

"This shouldn't have happened," Calder said, voice barely above a whisper.

"It wasn't your fault—"

He let out a sound that was half-laugh, half-snarl. I didn't think it was at me. It seemed more like it was at himself. At the trap.

He stood in Aoife's doorway, unmoving.

"Calder." I touched his arm. "She's going to be okay."

"I'm fine."

"You're not." His whole body was wound tight, like a bow string about to snap. "Talk to me."

He shook his head, jaw clenched. Whatever was eating at him went deeper than a trapped fox.

"She's going to be okay," I said again. "Aoife will—"

"Out." Aoife's voice cut through the moment like a blade. She stood in the doorway, apron smeared with blood, sleeves damp to the elbows. "Both of you. I need space if I'm going to save her."

"I can help," I started, but she was already shaking her head.

"You'll hover. He'll pace holes in my floor. Go walk it off."

Calder's jaw worked. He looked down at the fox, and something cracked in his expression. "If she—"

"I'll come get you if she takes a turn." Aoife's tone gentled just slightly. "She's stronger than she looks. Go."

For a moment, I thought he might refuse. His arms tightened around the small body, and I saw the war playing out across his face—the need to protect warring with the knowledge that he couldn't fix this with his hands.

Finally, carefully, he passed the fox to Aoife. His fingers lingered on her fur for just a second too long.

"Come on," I whispered, touching his elbow.

He nodded without looking at me. And followed me out into the morning that had started so perfectly and turned so sharp.

We made it maybe ten steps before he stopped walking entirely.

"I need some air," he said, but he was already turning away from me. "I'll... I'll find you later."

Before I could respond, he was heading toward the forest path that led away from the village. Away from me.

I stood there watching him disappear into the trees, my chest hollow. Whatever was wrong, he clearly didn't want my help figuring it out.

Fine. I had work to do anyway.

I STAYED in the charm shop longer than I needed to, half-heartedly moving things around, pretending I still had work to finish. I told myself I was being productive, but really, I was just waiting. Hoping he might come to me first, but he didn't.

So eventually, I gave in and went to him.

When I reached for the door, I hesitated. Just long enough to feel ridiculous. Then I knocked, two quick, quiet raps, and immediately regretted both of them.

What if I was reading this all wrong? What if this morning hadn't meant what I thought it did? What if—

The door opened, and Calder stood framed in the doorway. His hair was damp, half-tied at the back, with thin braids threaded through to hold the weight of it out of his face. His shirt was unlaced at the collar, sleeves shoved to his elbows. The bandage on his forearm looked clean, which was a relief.

For a second, he just looked at me, his thumb catching on a splinter in the doorframe. He worked it back and forth, as if it was easier than looking at me.

"Hi," he said, finally.

I took a small step forward without overthinking it and tilted my face up towards his slightly. It was almost exactly like I'd done this morning in the meadow. My body reacted to him before my brain could stop it. We were too new to say it was a habit, maybe it was just out of hope.

He didn't lean in.

I waited for another heartbeat, thinking maybe he just needed a moment to catch up to where I was. But his body language didn't soften. If anything, he seemed to pull further into himself.

Instead, his free hand flexed once at his side, fingers curling and releasing like he was fighting the impulse to reach for me. His eyes dropped to my mouth for half a second before snapping back up, and I caught the moment he made himself look away.

And just like that, I understood. Whatever that kiss had been this morning, it wasn't an open invitation for more. It could just as easily have been a mistake he would not repeat.

I cleared my throat, and took a step back, putting us at a more reasonable distance. "Sorry. I just...wanted to check in. I probably should have asked this morning about stopping by before I did it."

His brows tugged together, almost imperceptibly. "You don't need to do that."

"I just wanted to make sure you were okay. And the fox."

"She's with Aoife." He stepped back, enough for me to enter. "Come in."

I crossed the threshold, heart already unraveling in my chest. Everything felt different than it had a few hours ago. The easy way of just existing between us had cooled into something more careful, more distant. The inside of the workshop smelled like sawdust, pine oil, and something herbal that clung faintly to the air—probably whatever Aoife had sent him home with to care for the bite on his arm. The hearth had gone out completely, and the shutters were still drawn.

The room was quiet in a way that made the walls feel farther apart than they were. And mounted high on the far wall, above a shelf of wood stains and tools, was a sword.

The metal was dark and strangely veined, like something forged from more than just steel. The hilt was wrapped in worn leather, shaped for use, not for show. A weapon that had seen years of service — and still waited for more.

"That yours?" I asked, nodding toward it.

Calder's gaze followed mine to the sword. "It was my father's." A beat. "And his before him."

I waited for more, but he didn't offer it.

"It looks like it's seen use."

"It has."

That was all he gave me. I didn't ask anymore.

I knew the fox wasn't here, but I looked anyway—like part of me still expected her. Or needed something to look at that wasn't him.

"How is she?" I asked softly.

"I haven't heard anything," he said, wiping his hands on a rag. "I wish Aoife would have let me stay."

"You would've been in her way," I said.

"I know, she's not wrong," he murmured.

"How are you feeling? How's your arm?"

He shrugged, "I'll be fine."

He crossed to the bench and set the rag down, quiet and careful, like his body hadn't caught up to the conversation yet. Like he was still deciding what version of himself I'd come here to see.

"I didn't mean to interrupt anything," I said.

"You're not."

But he still wasn't looking at me. That quiet distance started to crawl under my skin.

"I saw your face this morning," I said. "When you saw that trap."

His shoulders tensed. He kept his focus on the far wall, like the sight of it was safer than looking at me. I couldn't tell if he was trying to protect me, or just didn't trust me with whatever he wasn't saying.

"You knew it wasn't for a fox," I continued. "Didn't you?"

Still nothing. I could feel the shift, the tightening of the air between us. The way he turned his head, slowly, until his eyes met mine.

"It wasn't set for something small," he said. "The teeth were too wide. Spacing was wrong. The clamp angle... it was designed to catch something bigger. Something strong."

"Then what was it for?"

Calder reached for a carving knife on his workbench, and beside it sat a block of ashwood, smooth on one side, the edges dulled by handling. He turned the blade in his palm once, then picked up the wood. He handled them absentmindedly, the motion more habit than intent.

He shook his head once. "It's hard to say."

"But you recognized it," I said, stepping closer. "You've seen traps like that before."

He didn't answer for a moment. Then finally: "Yes."

I held his gaze. "Outside the valley?"

He nodded.

"And this one wasn't outside," I said. "It was here. Set inside the wards."

His jaw clenched hard enough I saw the muscle tick in his cheek. He didn't deny it.

I stepped closer again, voice dropping. "How did someone even manage to place a trap like that? That brutal? *Inside* the wards? They're intent-based. They're not supposed to let anything through that means harm."

"And they didn't."

"So you're saying someone *here* set it. Someone who lives in Glenmere?"

Calder didn't answer at first. He just stood there, jaw tight, like the words were already sitting on his tongue but he hadn't decided whether to speak them or swallow them whole.

Then, finally, he said it.

"Yes."

The floor didn't fall out from under me, but the center of my chest hollowed out.

"Why?" I asked. "Why would someone do that?"

"I don't know," he said. "Not exactly."

"Then guess." My voice cracked on it. "You've clearly thought about it."

He let out a slow breath, and when he spoke again, it was quieter. More certain.

"They wanted something to get through."

I stared at him. "What does that mean?"

"There was tampering around that trap this morning. That wasn't the first time. There have been others. The others have all been smaller breaches though, barely noticeable. I didn't know what to make of them until I saw where the trap was set.

It wasn't just near the weak spot—it *was* the weak spot. That's where they've been concentrating. I think someone has been testing to see how far they could go."

"But why? Why sabotage the wards at all?"

"To let something in," he said. "Something big enough to scare people. Not destroy the village. Just... shake it. Make everyone look around and ask who failed to stop it."

And then I felt it, everything he couldn't bring himself to say to me.

My throat tightened. "You think they want to blame me."

He didn't say yes, but he didn't have to.

"They know you're tired," he said instead. "They know how much you've been carrying, and until very recently you've been carrying it alone. If something had gotten through, and people started pointing fingers... you wouldn't have been able to defend yourself. You'd be too busy trying to fix it."

I felt like I'd been struck.

"But that didn't happen," I said. "The wards held. We caught it."

Calder looked away.

"They didn't get through," I repeated, more urgently. "So why are you acting like something bad happened?"

He hesitated. "I think somebody thought they could set you up. They probably thought you'd be too distracted training me to notice small damages. That your attention would be split."

I stepped in front of him. "What are you talking about? What aren't you telling me?"

His jaw flexed. His hands curled into loose fists at his sides. But when he finally spoke, his voice was calm.

"There are more wards," he said. "Outside the ones you hold."

My stomach dropped. The trap hadn't failed because the saboteur was sloppy. It had failed because something else had stopped it. Calder had stopped it. The silence that followed rang in my ears.

"What?"

"Mine held," he said. "Yours—someone inside knew how to damage them. Enough tiny cuts from the inside, and the wall starts to fray. But they didn't know about mine. I've been reinforcing the outer perimeter," he said. "Quietly. Around the valley."

"You mean... outside the boundary?" My voice sounded far away. "There are new wards surrounding *my* wards?"

He nodded.

My heart was in my throat, its beat pounding through my head. "Since when?"

"Since I got here."

I didn't speak.

I couldn't.

Because there had been so many nights I'd dragged myself back from the edge of collapse—barely upright, barely breathing—believing I was the only one holding the valley together.

I'd let that belief carve itself into my bones. Every morning I woke up with my hands already shaking before my feet ever hit the floor. I once stitched a ward break in the middle of the night, with a fever so high I soaked through my clothes, because I thought I was the only thing standing between the village and a breach.

And he'd let me.

My voice, when it came, felt too small for the room. "You were reinforcing them. This whole time."

"Yes."

"You let me believe they were holding because of me."

His expression flickered, brows pulled together. "They were holding because of you," he said, voice tight. "I just— I didn't want you to carry the whole weight alone. I thought if I could take the first hit, soften the impact, then maybe you'd stop pushing yourself so hard. You were the army, Meira. I was only ever trying to be the front lines."

"No." I shook my head. "They weren't. Not the way I thought."

He didn't argue with me. That was almost worse.

I took a half step back, like distance might make any of this feel less sharp.

"You let me think I was failing," I whispered, the words shredded through the armor I wore around my heart. "You know, before you, before recently, I would stare at my ceiling every night, thinking I wasn't enough. Wondering if I had it in me to go out and do it again the next day. And all this time, I wasn't really alone out there. And you knew. You *knew*."

"I was trying to protect you."

I laughed, but it came out wrong—too raw to be anything close to amusement.

"Protect me?" I echoed. "Protect me how? By treating me like a threat to myself?"

"That's not what I meant. I didn't want to—"

"To what?" I snapped, the words coming out louder now, and as fast as I could hurl them at him. "Didn't want to help? Didn't want to share the weight? Or didn't want me to know *you* were carrying it at all?"

His mouth opened. Closed.

"Do you have any idea what it's been like?" I asked. "To hold this place together, day after day, with no backup? No one to tell me it was okay to stop? I've been tearing myself open to keep these wards alive, and you were out there patching the edges behind my back like I was a child playing pretend."

"I never thought that."

"Then what *did* you think?" I demanded. "What have you been telling yourself that made this okay?"

The silence that followed wasn't defensive. It was quiet in the way only guilt ever is.

When he finally spoke again, it was soft.

"I watched you carry more than anyone should have to. I thought if things were more secure, you might not work so hard. I just wanted to ease your burden."

"But you didn't," I said. "In fact, everything I've been carrying now feels even heavier. I've thought I was drowning for years, and all this time I had no reason to struggle as hard as I did?"

He nodded once. No argument. No excuse.

And that silence, that same infuriating quiet he always retreated into. It snapped inside me, a branch giving way under too much weight.

Because I'd trusted that this morning meant something. I'd trusted the way he looked at me. The way he touched me. The way he kissed me like I was already his.

But he hadn't trusted me.

Not with the truth. Not with the risk.

Not even with the wards.

I took a step back, then another. My hands were trembling, but I didn't try to hide it.

"I would've understood," I said quietly. "If you'd told me."

He looked up.

"I would've held the line with you."

And then I turned, and walked out before the weight of it could pull me to the floor.

"Meira—"

I stopped. Just for a second.

He'd crossed halfway toward me, one hand half-lifted like he might reach for my arm. But he didn't. He just stood there. Still not saying the one thing I needed to hear.

I didn't want an apology. I wanted to go back two years, to know that I hadn't been alone. I wanted to go back and know that he'd been there because he couldn't stand to watch me struggle alone, not because he thought I couldn't handle it.

I waited. Just long enough to know he wouldn't stop me.

And then I left, because I couldn't beg him to fight for me. I couldn't survive if he chose silence instead.

18

———

I didn't have anywhere to go.

The only thing I could think to do was find Sorcha. Drag her to the tavern, where I would sit her and Brenna down in the booth by the hearth, and tell them everything. And they would listen, nod, and be angry right alongside me.

I'd let it pour out in sharp, ugly waves. Every searing thought, every swallowed feeling, every time I'd bitten my tongue until it bled.

I'd tell them everything, about Calder and the wards.

I would drag every last piece out of me, let it cut and bleed and echo until the weight of it was theirs too.

They'd be furious, right alongside me. Sorcha would say *"He's an ass, Meira. You deserve better,"* and Brenna would pile on, cutting even sharper.

I wanted that. I wanted them to say it, to agree, to validate every shard of shame I couldn't pull from my skin.

I rehearsed it in my head. The lines I'd lead with. The brutal things I'd let myself say. The ones I wasn't brave enough to say to him.

But every version ended the same way: with Sorcha's face crumpling in sympathy. And me—furious at her for offering it.

But the second I pictured it—Sorcha's face, her mouth curling around those words—my whole chest recoiled.

Because it wouldn't help. I might feel better for a breath, but it wouldn't take long before that comfort turned to resentment. I'd hate her for saying it, because as mad as I was, I didn't believe it was true.

So I turned before I ever reached Sorcha's house, and took the long way home. Let the river path wind me back through the woods, back to the quiet. At least at home I could fall apart without anyone watching.

I'd walked this path with him once, and that memory made this time ache. Because back then, I hadn't been angry yet. I still believed the work I was doing mattered.

I was so godsdamned mad—at Calder, at myself, at the world—and still, I knew if anyone else tried to speak a word against him, I'd snap. I didn't want him defended, but I couldn't stand the thought of him being blamed, either.

That made me angrier than anything. That I still wanted to protect him, too.

I DIDN'T CRY when I got home. I sat at the table, on the floor, even in the doorway once. I just moved from place to place like a ghost.

For days, I didn't go to the wards. Didn't open the shop.

I just kept existing, one quiet hour at a time.

The worst part wasn't the silence. It was how easy it was to disappear inside it.

Another few days passed, at least, before I left the house.

If something horrible had happened, if every ward had failed, someone would have come to get me. The village would have sent runners, and the Council would have demanded answers.

But I hadn't heard from anyone, which meant he was still doing the work.

I dragged myself to the western boundary one morning, a cloak pulled over my nightgown. The sun hadn't crested the eastern ridge, and dew clung to every wildflower and blade of grass.

The wards hummed with stable magic. Clean, steady, and perfectly anchored.

I stood there staring at work that should have been mine, and felt rage start to boil over in my chest.

He wouldn't even let me fail properly.

I HADN'T EATEN. I wasn't even sure I had anything to eat, I couldn't remember the last time I'd gone to the market.

I must have tried to make tea, because the kettle was still full of water. The tea leaves I'd measured out sat untouched in a bowl near the sink.

At some point I'd set out a mug, but must have forgotten about it. It was days later when I realized it was sitting there, taking up space on the table. I thought about adding another, just in case.

I sat with my shoulders hunched, unfocused my eyes, and tried to think of nothing, but could only see the space Calder had left behind.

I was angry. I was angry and I didn't know where to put it. Angry that I was back in this house, back in this body, back in this silence like I'd never left it.

The mug hit the cabinet before I had time to stop myself from throwing it.

It shattered into shards and scattered across the floor, the pieces found their way under the oven and table. I didn't move.

I just stared at the pieces with my chest heaving and my pulse pounding in my ears.

And then I broke, too.

It wasn't a gentle break, I felt just as jagged as the ceramic all over the floor. I buried my face in the crook of my elbow at the kitchen table—where my mother used to slice apples, where my father used to drink his morning tea, where I'd had breakfast with Calder not so long ago—and sobbed until I could no longer breathe.

When I finally lifted my head, the cottage was still cold. Still dim. Still quiet. The silence didn't just feel empty anymore, now it felt dead.

The knock on the door was soft but certain. I didn't answer. I didn't move.

"Meira?"

Sorcha's voice was low and hesitant as she stepped inside. Brenna, who carried a large pot with something wrapped in linen balanced on top, followed. Neither of them smiled when they saw me. They just studied me.

"Hey," Brenna said softly. "We're here."

"You don't have to," I rasped. "I'm fine."

"You're not," Sorcha said, already crossing to the broken mug. She knelt and started gathering the pieces, careful not to cut herself.

"Don't," I said. "Just leave it."

"Absolutely not." Brenna joined her, sweeping the smaller shards into her palm.

They worked in quiet efficiency, cleaning up my mess and somehow, I didn't feel ashamed of it. When they were done, Sorcha sat across from me while Brenna moved to the hearth.

"Calder looks like someone kicked him in the ribs," Sorcha said after a while. Her back was to me. She said it like it was just a fact. "Saw him near the bakery yesterday. He looked like shit."

"He wouldn't say what happened," Brenna added as she ladled something thick and fragrant into a pot. "But when you disappear, and he looks like he's falling apart, we figured something happened."

"You don't have to tell us what happened," Sorcha said. "We just wanted to make sure you weren't sitting in here thinking no one noticed."

"I didn't want to bother anyone," I muttered.

"We wanted you to know we're here," Brenna said, lighting the fire. "We love you, Mer. You never have to hold yourself together for us."

I pressed the heel of my hand to my eyes.

"Just..." Sorcha paused. "If it's okay with you, we just want to be here."

I nodded. It wasn't much. But it was enough.

They settled into the room, and continued carrying on as if this could have been any one of the hundreds of nights we'd spent together doing nothing.

Brenna found where I kept the extra blankets and tossed one over the back of the couch. Sorcha opened windows to let in the breeze, then shut them again when she realized how chilly it was.

Someone reheated the tea I'd forgotten to make.

Someone else lit the candles.

They didn't treat me like glass. They just talked. About the garden party that got rained out, about Nolan's awful new haircut, about whether Aoife was secretly sweet on Old Thom, who brought her fresh bread every week and still called her "miss."

I didn't say much. Just listened. Let their voices fill the room.

Brenna stirred the stew she'd brought, and Sorcha braided my hair without asking. True to their word, they didn't press.

"I brought those nut biscuits you like," Brenna said after a moment. "Don't ask how many I ate on the way."

"I love those," I mumbled.

"We know," Sorcha said gently, sitting down beside me.

She looped her arm around my shoulders and tugged me in. She didn't let go.

And for the first time in days, I let my head rest on someone else's shoulder. Just for a minute.

They didn't try to fix anything, outside of the mess I'd made. They just stayed.

When they left hours later, the cottage was warm. The hearth glowed. The floor was clean.

For the first time in days, the silence didn't feel so much like abandonment, it just felt like space.

19

Three days passed since Brenna and Sorcha had staged their gentle intervention, and I was feeling steady enough to venture beyond my doorstep.

I was out of several necessities, and told myself I could face the market, that it would be good for me, and if nothing else, I needed fresh apples and new soap.

I'd forgotten how pretty the village could be in the morning. Early morning sunlight made everything more beautiful— window boxes spilling over with late summer blooms, the stones of cottage walls worn smooth by decades of weather, even the dust kicked up by an early cart heading to market caught my eye. I walked slowly, soaking it all in, in no hurry to break the haze of feeling almost normal again.

It was nice for a moment, to pretend I was just out to enjoy a peaceful morning.

I told myself I wasn't looking for him, but even as I tried to lose myself in the simple pleasure of being at the market, my heart kept hoping.

My eyes swept the market stalls anyway, checking corners and doorways. I hadn't seen Calder since our fight. The rational part of me knew he was probably avoiding anywhere I might be, I doubted he wanted to see me. The irrational part hoped he'd appear anyway.

The abundance of summer was displayed across vendor tables in rainbow piles of fat tomatoes, summer squash, and berries of every color. Shoppers browsed unhurriedly, taking their time in the way only summer allowed. The whole square smelled like fresh bread and Fern's cinnamon buns.

"Meira."

I turned to find Nolan walking towards me with his hands in his pockets. The expression on his face was almost sheepish, he looked more careful than he normally did. Careful or calculated.

"Nolan." I kept my voice neutral.

"Could I speak with you?" He stopped a respectful distance away, glancing around.

I waited, letting the awkwardness stretch until he broke the silence himself.

"I wanted to apologize for pushing you about the partnership. My uncle thought—well, it doesn't matter what he thought." Nolan ran a hand through his hair. "You've been carrying a lot alone, and that's obviously not sustainable."

It was an apology worded the only way he knew how, laced in condescension and delivered like he was doing me a favor.

"Alright," I said, my voice flat.

"The thing is," he continued, leaning closer to me, "I've been keeping an eye on the wards. For everyone's safety, you understand. And there have been... inconsistencies."

My posture went rigid. "What kind of inconsistencies?"

"Small things. Anchor points that seem to lose their connection. Weak spots are appearing more frequently." He met my eyes, and for a moment I almost believed the worry there. "I know you've been under a lot of pressure, and I hate to see you struggling. I thought maybe if we —"

"You thought what, exactly?"

Calder's voice came from my right, calm and conversational. I turned to see him approaching with that unhurried confidence, and despite everything between us, it was impossible to look anywhere else.

My heart ached at the sight of him. After everything that had happened between us, he was still here. Still protecting me. I didn't know if that made it better or worse.

Nolan's expression tightened, the careful concern slipping just enough to reveal something harder underneath. "I was expressing concern about ward stability."

"Were you." Calder stepped to my side, his attention fixed on Nolan with quiet intensity. "That's interesting. Because those inconsistencies you mentioned? That's exactly how I'd describe some of the tampering I've found recently."

"I don't know what you mean."

"Sure you do." Calder's tone remained perfectly reasonable. "Someone's been breaking thread connections right at the stone. Strange, unnatural fissures are forming in the most random places." He rolled his shoulders once, settling into his stance like he was getting comfortable for a long chat.

Nolan's nostrils flared.

"Meira and I found a fox caught in a trap near one of those wardbreaks. The trap had a three-branch sigil still visible on the iron."

My breath caught.

I hadn't even looked at the trap.

Calder had. Of course he had. He'd been calm, furious, focused. I'd been too caught up in the blood, the fox, the way his hands shook. But he'd seen it. He'd recognized it.

"I believe that mark belongs to the Birchwood's forge," Calder continued, his tone almost pleasant. "And I think... that's your mother's maiden name, if I'm not mistaken?"

The color drained from Nolan's face. "That's a serious accusation."

"It's a serious problem." Calder didn't raise his voice, he stayed solid and certain. "Here's what I think happened," Calder continued conversationally. "The Council wanted Meira partnered. You volunteered. Unfortunately, she wasn't interested in your proposal and chose differently. I admit I don't know you too well, but I have noticed you don't like when you don't get your way.

It wasn't going to be as easy as having Uncle Thomas sign a piece of paper anymore, but your desires weren't impossible. You see, if you could make it look like Meira and I were failing first, then you'd have a justification to argue the partnership."

"You can't prove—"

"I can," Calder said. "And if it happens again."

Nolan looked between us, jaw working. Then something shifted in his expression—the sheepish apology falling away entirely to reveal the calculation that had been there all along.

"The wards needed strengthening anyway," he said, voice hardening. "Everyone knows she's been stretched too thin. A few small failures would have proved the point without anyone getting hurt."

My stomach dropped. "Small failures?"

"Nothing dangerous," Nolan said, the only thing on his face now was cold practicality. "Just enough to show the Council that you needed support."

"That I was incompetent." The words tasted bitter.

"That you needed a partner. A *suitable* partner." He stepped closer, and I saw the man who'd watched me struggle just to be able to catalog my weaknesses. "Someone who could help with the wards, manage the shop properly, make sure everything runs the way it should."

He reached for my arm, but I recoiled on instinct.

The casual way he said *manage the shop* made my hands

curl into fists. As if everything I'd built, everything I'd inherited, was already sitting in his ledger. "I'd rather fail alone than owe you a single thing."

"With your magic and my leadership, we could've rebuilt everything stronger. Run the shop, manage the wards, stabilize the valley the way your parents would've wanted."

"Leave her alone, Nolan," Calder said.

He didn't raise his voice, but he didn't have to. The way he said the words made them feel like a threat.

The villagers nearest us had turned to watch.

Nolan bristled. "I beg your pardon?"

"You haven't," Calder said. "But you should."

But before Nolan could respond, Elder Muriel appeared beside us like she'd materialized from thin air, wearing her most diplomatic smile.

"Gentlemen," she said mildly. "Surely we're not going to have any issues in the middle of this beautiful market day?"

She looked between the three of us with sharp eyes that missed nothing, clearly having heard enough to understand exactly what was happening.

"Just a discussion about ward maintenance," Nolan said quickly, his political instincts kicking in.

"Mmm." Muriel's tone made it clear she wasn't buying it. "Well, whatever maintenance issues we're having, I'm sure they can be resolved without disturbing everyone in the square."

She turned that polite smile on me. "Speaking of things that need resolving—as we discussed, Lughnasadh is approaching rapidly, and we really must finalize the arrangements for your handfasting."

My throat went dry. "We haven't really started planning—"

"Which is exactly why we can't delay any longer. Lughnasadh would be perfect," Muriel continued smoothly. "We're already having a festival for the last celebration of the light season before autumn sets in. It would be lovely to add a hand-fasting ceremony to the festivities."

Handfastings and marriages were common at Lughnasadh, but the festival was less than two weeks away.

"The whole valley will be celebrating anyway," she added with a meaningful look at Nolan. "Now it will truly be a joyous occasion. Everyone can be together to witness your new beginnings."

Nolan's face had gone carefully blank, but I could see the calculation behind his eyes. A public handfasting. In front of everyone. Making it real in a way that couldn't be undone or questioned.

Calder was quiet for a moment, his gaze fixed somewhere in the distance. Then he looked at me.

"If that's what Meira wants," he said quietly, and the resignation in his voice was worse than any argument would have been. He wasn't going to stop me from choosing something that broke both our hearts, even if he wanted to.

"Wonderful!" Muriel turned to me expectantly. "I assume you agree?"

"That sounds fine," I heard myself say.

"Excellent!" Muriel bustled off, already making plans, leaving us in tense silence.

Nolan looked between Calder and me, something ugly flickering across his features as he walked away.

"Calder," I started.

"I should go," he said, already stepping back. "I have some work to finish."

I watched him walk away, disappearing between the stalls. Around me, it was like the village hadn't even paused, but I stood frozen in place

. . .

I HAD LESS than two weeks to figure out if Calder would stand beside me because he still wanted this, or if the bargain meant he didn't have a choice.

When I got home, I tried to throw the door shut behind me, like I could trap everything bad outside, but it stuck before it closed.

I yanked it open again, and slammed it twice as hard. It bounced off the warped frame and caught me square in the shoulder.

The door itself wasn't the problem. The cracked threshold Calder had pointed out the morning after dinner at Sorcha's, was now fully broken. Splintered and jutting, wedged like a bone out of joint.

I kicked the threshold to try to knock the stuck piece out of the way, but it didn't budge. I kicked harder, and when it didn't budge, I lost the last thread of control I'd been holding on to.

I kicked until the wood splintered and cracked, until my toes burned and the throb of pain was the only thing louder than my heartbeat. Until the rage in my chest had somewhere to go besides inward.

Tears were blurring my eyes, and I was breathing like I'd just run for my life. The broken piece had finally come free, but with it I had completely destroyed the bottom of the frame.

I wiped roughly at my eyes, took one deep, ragged breath, and went inside.

I shut the door with calm and careful hands. I let the quiet of the empty cottage take me. I leaned my back against the door, no longer possessing the strength to support myself, and slid against the wood until I hit the floor and folded in on myself completely.

I let my head fall into my hands, and I sobbed.

20

———

I didn't make it upstairs that night. I lit a single candle and stared at the flame until it drowned itself in wax. When the chill became unbearable, I pulled the blanket from the couch and collapsed right there, boots and all.

The next morning, I tried to pretend it hadn't happened.

I got up even earlier. Earlier than usual. Told myself I'd beat him to it today, that he'd done my job for me long enough, and that I'd handle the wards myself.

But by the time I reached the edge of the orchard, the stones were already glowing warm amber with new magic.

The next day, even though I'd left home early enough that the moon and stars were completely visible, it was the same story. He'd already done the work.

I stopped trying after the fourth day.

He wasn't doing it secretly, he just wasn't involving me.

He didn't knock like he did when we'd walk together, didn't leave notes about what he was doing. He didn't try to contact me at all, didn't try to make me talk.

He just kept the valley safe, quietly and without acknowledgement.

That was worse, somehow, that he still cared. That even after everything, even though I wasn't speaking to him, he wouldn't let me fall apart alone.

I stopped walking near the perimeter entirely. I knew exactly what I'd find, and I didn't need the reminder that he was better than I'd ever been.

Instead, I poured myself into my charm shop. I used my extra magic on charm orders, to get them caught up, delivered, and even scheduled in new ones. I filled the time by constantly moving, avoiding idle hands and the silence of being alone.

Avoided the gap under my door from the missing threshold I still hadn't fixed.

And then, a week after I'd stopped checking the wards, I woke before the sun to the sound of hammering.

Deliberate, controlled, and rhythmic hammering.

I moved slowly, and pulled the curtain back just far enough to see the crown of his head. Chestnut brown. Familiar. Bent over a cluster of tools on the porch.

Calder.

For one aching second, I forgot everything—the kiss, the fight, the silence that followed. I forgot about the years I worked myself to death, and how it hadn't meant a damn thing. My heart lurched, made happy and hopeful by just the sight of him.

And then I remembered.

Part of me wanted to rush down the stairs, throw open the front door and tell him to leave. Another part of me wanted to fall into him, to be held by him while I cried until I forgot why I ever hated him.

But I didn't do either.

Instead, I padded downstairs to light the stove, and let the kettle heat while I changed into an oversized tunic and tights. Then, with two sturdy mugs in the same hand, held by shaking fingers, I opened the door.

And there he was—kneeling, hammer in hand, finishing the last nail of the threshold I'd destroyed.

His head snapped up.

"Shit, Meira—did I wake you? I was trying to be quiet."

"No," I said. "I'm usually up by now."

He hesitated, then looked around. "Hope I didn't wake the neighbors."

"It's just Mrs. Blackwood next door. And if you had woken her, you could've just offered to let her pet your forearms. She would've forgiven you immediately."

He blinked. Then he let out a laugh so sudden and full, I sloshed some of the hot tea over the side of the mugs when I startled. I looked down at the spill on the porch. "That might have done it. You'd better go ahead and roll up your sleeves," I teased.

He smiled, wide and unguarded and warm, and for the first time in days, every hollow place in my heart was filled with light.

I handed him a cup. He took it carefully and wordlessly, then moved to sit with his back against the front door.

I sat beside him. Close enough to feel his warmth without touching. Whatever I was feeling now, it wasn't strong enough to keep much space between us.

We each faced forward and sipped in silence for a few moments.

Birdsong filled the silence between us. I'd never been uncomfortable in the quiet moments between Calder and me, and even with the time apart, we'd kept that familiarity.

I told myself I'd listen to whatever he had to say if he wanted to speak, but I wouldn't be the first to break the quiet.

Eventually, he did.

"I took care of the wards this morning."

"You've been taking care of the wards every morning," I said. I'd only meant since we'd stop doing them together, to reference that I knew he'd been handling it on his own. But by the way he winced, he'd taken it as a jab.

He thought I'd been referring to *those* wards, the ones he'd hidden from me.

Calder set his cup down on the porch, and wiped his palms on the legs of his pants.

"Meira," he said, and rubbed the back of his neck like he didn't know what else to do with his hands. "I've been meaning to say this for a long time. I'm sorry."

He let out a long breath. "I don't want to make excuses. I was wrong from the beginning. I had no right to supersede your work, especially not without telling you."

His voice was steady, but soft and careful, as if he wasn't sure how to put his thoughts into words.

"It was stupid. I convinced myself I was doing it for you. I told myself that I wasn't usurping you, but that these new wards—what I was doing—would be your front lines. I did it to make your life easier.

I thought if you saw that nothing was getting through, you'd stop pushing yourself so hard. That you'd give less and less, and eventually you might take a break, come up for air. And when you did, I'd tell you."

His eyes flicked toward mine, waiting for any hint of argument from me, but I didn't speak.

"But you never did, Meira. You just kept giving, more and more. And I hadn't realized—" He shook his head. "I hadn't realized how much you'd already sacrificed, or how much you still would."

I didn't know anybody even noticed me.

"I came to Glenmere, almost by accident," he said. "I'd been near the valley in the past—a few months before—but hadn't come this way with Glenmere in mind. When I realized where I was going, which way I was headed, I thought I'd try to catch up with your parents."

My fingers tightened around my mug until my knuckles turned white.

"I'd spoken to them several times. Even shadowed them as they worked. I've been to a lot of places and seen a lot of things, Meira. But I'd never seen anything like this. This system they'd helped build and shape, the sophistication of the protections—well, Forest Fae have shields and wards, but nothing like this."

Blood roared through my ears. The thumping was deafening. I couldn't get any air into my lungs.

"Life outside of Glenmere is different. Forest fae might be the typical outcasts, but even within other cities or villages, none are quite like Glenmere."

I just stared straight ahead, chest heaving.

"There are countless ways this valley is unique," he went on. "But one thing that I've yet to find anywhere else is the togetherness. Everywhere else is... individualistic. No one burdens themselves with more than what belongs to them."

He paused. "Here, it's different. Your parents showed me that."

Pain twisted sharp and slow inside my chest.

"I ran into them near the southern stone," he said. "I don't know what made me approach them. I almost didn't, you never really know how you'll be received between another kind of fae, but they were gracious and kind."

He looked down at his clasped hands. "I asked them what they were doing, and they offered to walk me through the whole system. I watched them cast new patches and anchor fresh lines. The care they put into their work, this work wasn't just functional to them, it was sacred.

Your parents devoted their lives to creating this protection for the people of this village, and they had to do it daily. I'd never heard of such a thing before. They worked so hard and stayed rooted so as to protect people who weren't even their family.

I admired and envied that so much."

He'd known them.

This quiet, selfless outsider—this male who'd likely saved my life two years ago—hadn't been a stranger to my parents. He'd *known* them. Learned from them. *Envied* them.

And I hadn't even known he existed.

"Meira, that day I found you at the wards—" His voice cracked. He cleared his throat.

"When I first walked into Glenmere, I hadn't meant to end up here. I'd just come through one of the hardest period of my life and needed to get away. So I walked. I walked and walked, and somewhere along the way, I thought about your parents. Maybe I could apprentice under them for a while. Maybe I'd find a purpose like they had. I needed my life—my work—to mean something.

"So without having a real plan, I walked right into the valley. And as I neared the northern wardstone, I saw a heap on the ground."

Calder ran a hand down his face and sighed. "I felt a kind of fear I'd only ever felt once before.

I remember thinking I was too late.."

Goosebumps erupted across every part of my skin.

"I saw blood on your face, and didn't hesitate. I picked you up and started toward the village. I don't even know how to explain the relief when I felt you breathing. I had no idea what had happened to you, didn't know if you'd been attacked, or cursed, or... I just didn't know.

Luckily, Aoife saw me carrying you across the meadow before I even reached her house. I didn't know she was a healer then, but she saw me carrying you and knew you'd drained yourself."

He rubbed his palms over his thighs. "I didn't want to leave. I *refused* to leave, once I knew who you were. Once I found out what you'd lost."

"What do you mean?" My voice came out thin. "She told you about my parents dying?"

Calder nodded slowly before he said, "She told me you'd just started working on the wards. I asked about the others—your parents—before I knew who they were to you, and she told me you'd just lost them. I didn't ask for details. I think not knowing made it easier to pretend it wasn't real."

I watched as anguish settled over his features.

"Then she told me that you were their daughter, and I felt like I knew that already, somehow. Your parents would tell me about you, things like your progress on the charm shop. They were so proud of you.

And I thought: this is where I'm meant to be. I had come here with the intention of helping your parents, and here was my chance. They weren't here anymore, and yet I was still going to be able to help them, because I could help you."

I had to bite my tongue so as to not interrupt him. Tears blurred my vision.

A few escaped Calder's eyes, and rolled down his cheeks.

"I went to the Council immediately. Aoife had told me enough, that I thought surely, if they knew I could help you, they'd let me. I went to them and told them everything. Told them I already knew some of it because your parents had taught me. But they said no. I couldn't understand, and they had no time or patience to entertain my questions.

"I went back to Aoife's, and she said they likely just didn't know me well enough. They didn't want me having direct access to their protections. It made sense. They didn't know me at all.

"So I went back to them a second time. I offered to at least accompany you. I pleaded with them to assign me to walk guard with my damn sword. I didn't ever want to use that damned thing again, but if it meant helping you, I would do it. I had it in my head that taking care of you — of lightening the load so you didn't pass out again — that was the goal.

"I never stopped to think about what *you* might want, how you might feel about this. Some primitive part of me just knew I couldn't let this happen ever again.

"Days turned to weeks, and I just decided I would make my own. I'd go outside your wards as far as I had to, and I'd encase them. I'd give you an extra layer of defense."

He met my eyes. "At the time, it made perfect sense."

I blinked slowly, chasing away tears, and reached for his hand. He let me take it, and wrapped his fingers around mine. I had meant to comfort him, but as always, he was the one taking care of me.

"Getting to know you, seeing how horribly I'd failed... I realized that by reinforcing the wards, I've been reinforcing my own peace of mind, but by not being honest with you, it was at the cost of yours."

"You knew them," I whispered. It barely made it past my lips. "And you've been here this whole time, and I never even —" I pressed my lips together, closed my eyes, and breathed only as deep as I could without crying.

The thought had crossed my mind in the past, that I'd never get to introduce him to my parents. I didn't know how to hold all of the grief of missing them, and gratitude that someone else had loved them too, the strange comfort of knowing they'd already met him.

21

I leaned into him then, and let my head rest against his arm.

To my relief, he didn't pull away.

I wanted so badly to take the weight from him—this guilt, this grief—but I didn't know how. All I could do was press our joined hands to my lips, slow and deliberate, a gesture that I hoped said, *I see you. I see you and I'm still here.*

In answer, he breathed a kiss onto the crown of my head.

We sat like that, pressed together, for a long, wordless moment. The air between us was no longer thick with pain, but had dulled into a quiet kind of ache. The sore and yellow healing of a bruise.

Then came the squeal—shrill, deafening, and unmistakable.

I stiffened. Calder froze beside me.

"What was that?" he asked in muted panic.

I leaned forward as far as I could from where I sat and peeked around the side of the porch. The morning sun had crept up behind the ridge, and the first signs of village life were beginning to stir.

"Mrs. Blackwood," I whispered. "She's opening all her windows. If she catches us out here, you're definitely getting petted."

He lunged for his tools, gathering everything he'd brought, with the swiftness of a thief mid-heist. I watched from where I'd been sitting, and covered my mouth to muffle my laughter. "What are you still doing down there?" He hissed. "We have to move!"

I almost cackled. The urgency in his voice, the scrabble of his boots as he gathered his things. I scooped up our mugs and carefully opened the door, mindful of its new frame, motioning him inside before the flirty old woman next door caught sight of him.

We crawled across the floor into the house, and when the door closed with a click, we grinned at each other like we'd just gotten away with something.

I walked through the living space and set the mugs in the sink. Calder kicked his boots off at the door like it was second nature. When he turned back, our eyes met—and for a moment, we just stood there, and I drank him in.

There was still something unresolved in the air between us. I still had so many unanswered questions, but the weight of it was lighter now. We weren't standing on opposite sides of it anymore. It would take time, but for now we had a truce.

His stomach growled.

It sounded loud in the quiet kitchen, and it made me realize how long the morning had already been. Most of the valley fae were likely just starting their days, and ours had already been so heavy, so hungry.

"I can make breakfast," I said, finally breaking the silence. "As a thank you. For fixing the door."

He looked down at his sleeves, unrolling and re-rolling them. Likely just something to do with his hands. "You don't owe me anything."

"Then what if I just want to?" I asked, already lighting the stove. "What if I ask you to let me make you breakfast because I'd like to?"

A pause.

Then, softly, Calder replied. "Then I'd like that."

"Okay then." I gave him a warm smile, hoping to ease some of the tension he was carrying in his shoulders.

He made his way into the kitchen and leaned against the counter. I moved toward the cupboard. The sun had crested the mountains now, and light fell across his features. His eyes almost glittered.

I liked seeing him in my space. I thought for a moment that this was the first time he'd been here, but then I remembered how he'd stayed over, when he'd carried me home after I collapsed at Sorcha's wedding.

I cracked several eggs into the iron skillet, added a pinch of salt and pepper, and stirred them slowly, scraping the bottom of the pan as they cooked. The stove gave off just enough heat that it warmed the kitchen, fighting off the chill from the morning air.

Calder inched closer, and leaned against the counter beside me, closer without hovering. He crossed his arms loosely. His presence was as it has always been, solid and still. Being this close to him for the first time in more than a week, I reveled in his cedar scent.

"Do you want toast?" I asked.

"Does it come with honey?"

"I have honey or, let's see," I maneuvered him away from the cabinet so I could rummage through it. "Honey or Aoife's rose hip jam."

He gave a low hum, approving. "So you're the one taking all the good jam. I tried getting another jar from her and she told me she was out for the season."

"I try to draw it out every year, I'm cautious and stingy with it so I can savor it for as long as possible."

"That's your first jar? I ate through my first jar in less than a week," he said.

"What do you mean is this my 'first jar'? How many did you eat before she finally turned you away?" I asked, pointing a fork at him in mock anger.

"I only had three this season, but I—"

"Three!" I shouted in disbelief. "Aoife gave you three jars?" I looked down and shook my head. "I thought she liked me."

"She probably likes you just fine," Calder said. "It's just that she can only have *one* favorite."

"This is unbelievable. And to think, I was starting to come back around to you before this."

I'd meant it as a joke, but he flinched all the same.

"Fine," I sighed, "I've already come back around to you. Just know there's a jam jar sized wedge still between us."

He huffed out a laugh, and I felt less like an ass.

We fell into a rhythm that felt impossibly normal. I finished with the eggs and toasted the bread, and he pulled down plates. I filled two mugs with fresh tea, he got the butter. It felt so normal, it could have been something we did all of the time, like we knew how to work together instinctively.

After I plated the food, he carried them to the table where we sat across from one another. The sunlight poured through the kitchen windows now, the warmth seeped into me in every place it touched my skin.

"Are your eggs okay?" I asked after we'd each had a few bites.

"Very good, thank you," he said around a bite of toast.

"How's the fox doing? Has Aoife released it yet?" I'd almost forgotten about his rescue. I looked for signs of its bite on his arm, but his skin was unblemished.

A soft smile tugged at the corners of his mouth. "She's good. Aoife says it's mostly healed, she just needs to stay off of her leg for a while still before she'll be ready to go back out to the meadow. Aoife says she wants 'that damn fox' out of her hair, but she refuses to let me take over the treatment. I think she's fallen in love."

"That sounds like Aoife," I said, smiling. "As long as she's at least a little bit mean, you know she likes you. It's when she's too polite that you know you're in trouble."

Calder let out a soft laugh. "She scolded me three times in the span of about ten minutes yesterday. I think that means I'm practically family now."

I nodded in agreement. "That's impressive. It took several years before Aoife warmed up to me."

"I'm just lucky, I guess."

"I think it's probably more about your charm than your luck," I said, and realized too late how it sounded. Calder quirked up an eyebrow. "Or, you know, your forearms."

He laughed at that, and when the last bites of our toast were gone, we again fell into sync as we moved into the kitchen. I filled the sink with soap and water to wash the dishes, and he was right behind me.

"I'll dry," he said, and reached for a towel that was hanging on a cabinet handle.

"You don't have to do that."

"I want to," he said. So I let him.

We moved around each other without effort again, seamlessly working together as if we'd done it a dozen times. I washed and rinsed, he dried and put away. It was the most innocent of things, washing dishes together, but the simple domesticity of it felt intimate all the same.

When we'd finished, I watched as his gaze shifted to the windowsill above the sink, and caught on the neglected adolescent plants Aoife had given me, still in their tiny ceramic pots.

Each one was wilted, their leaves browned and brittle,

indistinguishable from one another. I'd forgotten about them entirely.

"What happened here?" he asked gently, reaching a hand out toward them.

"I forgot," I said, wincing. "Aoife gave me those weeks ago. I kept meaning to plant them, but I guess they slipped my mind."

Calder held one of the brittle leaves gingerly between his fingers and then, right before my eyes, the color changed. Slow and subtle, like the rising of dawn, soft greens replaced the sallow stems. I watched as life spread back through the plant until its now-lush leaves reached for the light.

Brenna had told me once that forest fae were more attuned to nature. I hadn't realized she meant it quite so literally. All I could do was watch, mesmerized, as Calder renewed the life of each of the plants.

"I'll get those in the ground soon," I promised. I didn't want him to think I'd waste the effort he'd just put back into them, though it didn't look like it took any more energy from him than it would for him to snap his fingers.

"Do you have a place for them?" he asked.

Feeling somewhat ashamed, I shrugged. "Sort of. My mother had a garden so there's a plot where one *used* to be out there." I gestured to the back of the house. "But I've not touched it since she passed. It probably needs a lot of work before I can plant them."

"I can do that," he offered.

"I think you've done more than your fair share of favors for me today."

"Okay then," he conceded, "then how about I help."

"You don't need to help me," I said quietly.

"I'd like to," he replied, just as soft.

There wasn't a part of me that didn't want him to stay.

The way he said it—*I'd like to.* It didn't feel like this was about tending and planting a garden. Letting him stay felt like letting him back in, even if neither of us had said it out loud.

I didn't know if I was ready for that, but I wanted to be.

"If you're sure," I said.

"I'm sure."

CALDER DIDN'T WAIT for me to lead the way. He grabbed his boots from beside the front door, carried them through the kitchen, and slipped them on as he followed me out the back.

The air felt warmer now that the sun was higher in the sky, but the grass was still heavy with dew. It sparkled across the yard like stars.

The garden hadn't been touched since my mother died. Overgrown grass had crept in from all sides, swallowing the stone path that once led to her favorite place. The wooden borders had rotted through in places, but the bones of it were still there. At least we could see the shape of what it had been to give us some direction on what it might become.

Calder stood at the edge of it, hands on his hips, taking it all in. He walked the perimeter and let out the occasional "hmm."

"I should never have let it come to this," I said quietly. "It would break my mother's heart to see it now. She loved this place."

I stared down at the path, at the weeds that had cracked through the stones in the time I'd given up.

He crouched at a corner where two of the half-buried borders met, and lifted one away before throwing it aside. He tossed the other in the start of a pile, before he rose.

"Then we'll give it back to her. Piece by piece," he said, dusting the muddy soil off his hands.

The words filled every crack still remaining in my chest.

"I couldn't do it before," I said. "It's not just a bunch of weeds out here. It's—" I broke off. Grief, guilt, shame—they had all tangled together when I buried them inside myself.

Calder crouched at the edge of the garden again, and pressed one palm into the soil. He cocked his head slightly, like he was listening for something.

"I think sometimes we stop taking care of things... not because they didn't matter." He paused, and tore a handful of weeds from the earth, root and all. "But because they *did*. And we don't know how to look at them, or even be in the presence of them, without hurting."

Yes, I thought, *that's exactly how it feels*. But it also feels like my ribs are caving in, cutting into my lungs and I can't breathe enough to speak the words.

"There used to be a grove near where I grew up," he said, without looking up. Still pulling weeds. "It was close enough to the house that my parents let my sister and I play out there by ourselves, as long as we stayed together.

"There was a circular clearing beneath the trees, and we wore the grass down playing out there. With the tree canopy overhead, it felt like a little hideout.

"For years, we spent every waking moment out there. It's where we learned to climb trees and shoot a bow and arrow.

"One summer, my mother and sister planted all kinds of flowers around the circle. I don't know what they were, but there were tons of them in every color. My sister would cut them to bring inside, she loved having flowers in the house."

He paused. Turned a clump of roots over in his hand.

"Sylvie died before her thirteenth birthday. And after she died, I never went back to the grove. My parents didn't either. Not once. I held out a little bit of hope that my mother might still plant flowers the next summer. But she didn't, and we let the whole thing go wild. I think we were afraid to be reminded of what wouldn't be there."

He dropped the root, and watched the dirt scatter.

My throat closed. A sister. He'd had a sister, and she'd died so young. I wanted to reach for him, to say something, but he kept talking like he needed to get it all out before he lost his nerve.

"Losing my sister was hard on all of us, but it broke my mother. In the early days, when the pain was still too fresh, I cut some of the flowers that grew against the back of the house and brought them inside. I thought that because it had always made Sylvie so happy, they would make her happy too."

My heart ached for the younger version of him.

"It didn't," he said, finally looking at me, "She struck me. The first and only time in my life, but she did. I was more shocked than anything, and I would have ignored it entirely, except that she immediately crumpled to the floor. I tried my best to comfort her, but she sent me away."

I could see it all too clearly. Calder as a boy, maybe even a gangly young teenager, placing a handful of blooms in a glass of water. Being so proud of himself, trying to fix something unfixable.

"She apologized to me the next day, and she told me that seeing those flowers on the table, and realizing Sylvie wasn't the one who put them there, felt like she'd lost her all over again.

"That has never stopped haunting me.

"I *knew* Sylvie, and she would have hated that we never brought flowers in the house. I think it would have broken her heart that there was never a summer when we planted her flowers again.

"My mother seemed to think avoiding all reminders of Sylvie would make the loss of her easier to bear. But to me, not remembering Sylvie felt the same as trying to forget her, and forgetting Sylvie hurt worse."

He took a long, slow breath. "I only knew your mother for a little while, but I don't think she would want you to feel guilty. I think she'd love that you were in her garden, and I think she would want you to come back. Whenever you were ready."

The tears in my eyes felt like kindling with how much they burned.

"My mother got sick out of nowhere," I said, finally. "She was fine one week, and the next, she wasn't. Aoife still doesn't know what caused it, it moved too fast."

Calder reached like he might put his arm around me, but when he remembered his dirt covered hands, he held my equally dirty hand instead.

"She was gone within a couple of days," I said. "And then my father...there wasn't even anything wrong with my father."

I could still see the way he looked sitting by her bed after she passed. "It was like when she was gone, he went with her. Physically he was here, alive and breathing, but who he was, the soul inside of him left."

My throat tightened, but I kept going. "I think it was the next day, but it's hard to remember, so many of those early days are a blur. Too soon after we lost my mother, I came downstairs and he was completely still. Aoife told me that it happens sometimes—two people can't be apart, their bond is too deep."

Calder tugged lightly on my hand, offering to pull me into him. I wrapped my arms around his waist, and let myself melt into his chest. The tears were too fast to stop, thick and hot. I didn't even try to wipe them away.

I don't know how long we stood like that, tangled up in each other. He rubbed my back long enough that my breathing slowed, and the ache in my throat softened enough that I could speak.

"I miss them," I whispered. "I miss them so much some days that I feel sick. Still. And I've been sad, of course, I've been sad."

He pulled me even closer into him.

"Do you want to know how horrible I am? I'm angry that

my mother got sick and that no one could stop it, but I've also been angry with *them*."

He stilled but didn't let go of me. He even held his breath, I felt his chest still below my cheek.

"I'm angry that they left. I'm angry that I was the one left to be responsible for everything that was theirs. I'm angry that there was no plan, no letter, no *nothing*. Just me. Alone. With a village to protect and a legacy I never asked for." Hearing myself say it out loud, it sounded even more childish than it felt.

"I'm angry that they left me alone, that they didn't *try* to stay." My voice cracked on the word *try* like some part of me still couldn't believe it hadn't been enough.

"I know getting sick wasn't a choice. I *know* that." But my eyes burned hotter, my lips trembled despite the stubborn set of my jaw. I pulled back enough to look at him.

"I told you once about the story my father used to tell me," I said, barely above a whisper. "How he and my mother were made from the same dust. How they loved each other so much they swore their bones recognized it.

"I want that. Of course I do. I want to believe in that kind of love. But if my own father could leave me that easily, did he not love me enough to stay for me?"

Calder didn't speak, he just looked at me like he could feel every fracture in my chest.

"I've tried so hard to be enough. For everyone. I do the work, I carry the weight, I hold it all together. And sometimes I think that's the only reason anyone keeps me around."

I looked down at my hands—dirt-streaked, trembling. "Because I'm useful. Because I fix things. Because I make life easier."

Each word was a thorn in my throat.

"I don't even feel like a real person sometimes. Sometimes it just feels like I exist to cater to everyone around me. But if I didn't anymore, if I couldn't, would anyone even want me around?"

The wind shifted around us, just enough to lift the scent of soil and torn weeds. A cloud passed over the sun, temporarily casting us in shadow. The silence stretched so long I started to regret saying anything at all.

"I would."

I shook my head, already bracing for platitudes. I couldn't look at him. *Don't pity me, Calder.*

But he didn't waver.

"I'm not here because you're useful, Meira. I'm here because you have this spirit that just—" his brows furrowed, like he was trying hard to find the words. "Even when you're hurting, even when you're furious with the world, you still show up. You still care. You still look at the worst things and try to make them better. You make everything seem possible. I think you could do absolutely anything you put your mind to."

He hooked a finger under my chin and tilted my head so that I'd meet his eyes. "But that doesn't mean you have to."

My insides splintered.

"You don't have to *do* anything for me to stay."

I clenched my jaw and tried to swallow the lump in my throat back down.

"You don't have to be strong. You don't have to earn it. You don't have to fix a single thing. I'm not staying because you make life easier. I'm staying because it's *you*, even when it's hard."

My chest ached with all the things I wanted to believe, things I wanted to say but couldn't. From the way he looked at me, I knew his heart felt just as flayed as mine. I couldn't keep looking at him without crying, and I *really* did not want to cry.

So instead, I said, "You don't have to promise me to stay forever. Just... don't leave before the garden's done."

For a second, he didn't react. Still holding my chin up, he scanned my face, looking for any other fissure.

Then he smiled, and my insides felt like kindling.

He pressed a kiss to the top of my head, crouched down next to the weeds, and got to work.

So I did too.

We passed tools back and forth, pulled weeds, tilled the soil, and held up each worm we found like it was a prize.

And somewhere between the laughter and the dirt under my nails, between the sun warming my shoulders and the ache building in my arms, I remembered: This is what my parents used to do.

Not just the gardening, but *this*. The quiet joy they shared, and ease of togetherness. The work that didn't feel like work. I used to watch them from the kitchen window and wonder how something so ordinary could make them so happy.

Now I knew.

WHEN THE SUN reached its peak, I stood and stretched, wiping my hands on my thighs. Calder smiled up from where he was crouched beside the rosemary, dirt streaked across his face and arms.

"Thank you," I said. "For helping me with this. For—" I looked over the cleared plot, the neat rows we'd made. "For giving it back to me."

"Thank you for letting me."

I stepped closer, close enough to see the gold flecks in his eyes, the way his shirt clung to his shoulders. He stood slowly, brushing dirt off his hands, and I felt that familiar pull in my chest. It wasn't the desperate need from weeks ago, but steadier somehow.

The morning had stripped us both raw, left us standing with our hearts in our hands. And now, with dirt under our nails and the sun warming our backs, I realized I was tired of being careful.

I was tired of holding back as if that was going to keep me safe. I could live through the uncertainty of loving him. I couldn't survive knowing I'd never tried.

"I don't want you to leave," I said, the words coming easier than I expected. "Not just for the garden. I don't want you to leave at all."

He threaded his fingers through mine.

"I want you to stay." I took a deep breath. "I want you to stay for me."

He leaned down and pressed a soft kiss to my forehead. "I want to stay," he whispered against my skin.

When he pulled back to look at me, I didn't let him get far. I reached up and traced my thumb along his jaw, feeling the slight roughness of stubble.

"Come inside with me," I whispered.

His gaze dropped to my mouth, then back to my eyes. "Are you sure?"

I nodded, not trusting my voice. Because I was. For the first time in weeks, I was sure of something.

22

———————

I found Calder at his workshop, bent over a piece of wood that looked like it might become a chair leg. Wood shavings clung to his hair, and there was that line of concentration between his brows that I never got tired of watching.

"I have a surprise for you," I said from the doorway.

He looked up. "What kind of surprise?"

"The kind you have to come with me to see."

A smile tugged at the corner of his mouth as he brushed wood shavings from his hands. "Should I be worried?"

"Only if you don't like cute things."

He was already setting down his tools.

I didn't tell him where we were going, just took his hand and pulled him through the village. His fingers were rough from work, and I loved how familiar they felt to me now.

When we reached Aoife's cottage, I knocked once before pushing open the door.

"She's in the sitting room," Aoife called from the kitchen. "She's been waiting."

Calder's steps slowed as we entered the room. There, curled in a basket near the hearth, was the fox. Her russet fur gleamed in the low firelight, and when she saw Calder, her ears perked up and she made a soft chittering sound.

The expression on his face was pure, unguarded joy.

He crouched beside the basket, and she immediately pawed at his arms. I watched his face as he ran gentle fingers over her healed leg, watching her movement.

"She's perfect," he whispered, and she climbed fully onto his lap.

"Gods, she's tiny," he said, cradling her carefully. "She must have been just a kit when we found her."

"Still is, really," Aoife said. "I'm not convinced she was old enough to be on her own when you found her."

He was so careful with her, like she was made of spun glass. I wondered if he knew how gentle he was, or if it just came naturally to him.

"Thought you two might like to release her," Aoife said, appearing in the doorway. "She's been healed for days. Every time I try to shoo her outside, she just stares at me."

The walk to the eastern meadow was quiet, but I could feel Calder's reluctance with every step. When he said, "I know we have to let her go..." and trailed off without finishing, I realized I felt the same way.

When we reached the spot where we'd found her, Calder knelt and gently set her on the ground. She looked around, nose twitching, then sat down and stared up at us expectantly.

"Go on," I said softly. "You're free."

She tilted her head, then padded over to sniff my boots.

We tried walking away. She followed. We tried encouraging her toward the trees. She sat down and began grooming her paw. After twenty minutes of failed attempts, we gave up and decided to walk through the meadow, hoping she'd find something that reminded her this was home.

"She knows what she wants," I said, watching her trot back to us. "She's not going anywhere."

He looked as hopeful as I felt.

We made it all the way through the meadow, past the river, and halfway to Calder's workshop with her at our heels. By the time we reached his door, she was winding between our legs like a cat.

"Maybe we should just try again tomorrow," Calder offered, but he was already scooping her up.

I looked at him holding the fox, both of them looking perfectly content. "We could try tomorrow."

We both knew we were full of shit.

An hour later, we were sprawled on Calder's couch, the fox —Kit, as we'd started calling her—curled between us. She'd claimed the perfect spot where both our hands could reach her, and was purring.

"The handfasting is in a few days," I said tentatively.

"I know." He squeezed my hand.

I studied his profile in the firelight. "Do you still want to go through with it?" The question left my mouth before I could stop it, like some part of me still didn't believe I got to have this.

He turned to look at me fully. "Meira, when I agreed to this months ago, even in that chamber with the Council watching, I was all in."

"You were?"

He was quiet for a moment, thumb tracing over my knuckles. "My magic is different than yours," he said carefully. "If I say something, it becomes the truth. It's as good as a vow, and it doesn't need blood, or witnesses, or ceremonies. The old magic hears them, it listens, and I am bound by any promise I make."

His voice got quieter. "When I said our magics were compatible in that chamber, when I let them think we were courting— that wasn't just me getting us out of trouble. That was me choosing you."

It felt like I'd swallowed a cinnamon bun whole.

"Every time I showed up after that, every time I stayed—

that was the same choice, over and over. I meant it, Meira. Even if I didn't say the words with my hands tied to yours."

I watched him pet Kit, watched the fire dance in his eyes. "Well," I said finally. "At least one of us knew what we were doing."

He laughed, the sound rich and unguarded. I reached up to cup his jaw, turning his face toward me so I could kiss him properly. He pulled me closer until I was tucked against his side.

We fell quiet again, the only sounds Kit's contented purring and the crackle of the fire. I was half-dozing when Calder's voice broke the silence.

"Are you having second thoughts?"

I opened my eyes to find him watching me.

"Not a single one," I said.

Kit opened one golden eye, looked between us, then settled deeper into her spot with a satisfied sigh.

Apparently, she wasn't having second thoughts either.

23

———

I woke to sunlight streaming through the windows and an empty bed that felt too big without Calder in it. We'd agreed to spend the night apart, he'd mentioned something about tradition and anticipation, but now I was regretting how easily I'd agreed to it. The cottage felt unnaturally quiet without his steady breathing beside me, without Kit purring between us.

My stomach fluttered with nerves.In a few hours, I'd be standing in front of the entire valley, binding myself to him officially. Publicly. Permanently.

I touched the pillow where his head usually rested, and still smiling like a fool, forced myself out of bed.

The kettle was just starting to whistle when familiar voices drifted through the front door, followed by the sound of someone trying to knock while clearly carrying too much.

"Meira! Open up! My arms are going to fall off!"

I opened the door to find Sorcha juggling a bundle of white fabric, a basket of what looked like cosmetics, and at least three bottles of wine. Brenna stood behind her with her own collection of oddities, grinning like she'd been planning this assault for weeks.

"Happy handfasting day!" Sorcha announced, bustling past me into the cottage.

"It's barely past dawn," I protested, but I was already smiling. "How are you both so awake?"

"Pure excitement," Brenna said, setting her bag on the kitchen table with a satisfied thump. "Plus, Sorcha's been up since yesterday planning this."

"Since yesterday?"

Sorcha was already shaking out the bundle she'd been carrying. It was her own wedding dress, but it had been altered. The neckline was different, lower maybe, and there was delicate embroidery around the sleeves that I knew hadn't been there before.

"You didn't," I breathed.

"Oh, I did." She held it up against me, eyes bright and proud. "I couldn't let my best friend get handfasted in just any dress. Besides, this way the dress gets to see another perfect day."

It was too early for this, but my throat tightened anyway. "Sorcha..."

"Don't you dare cry yet," she warned. "Brenna has been practicing makeup on me all week, and I refuse to let your red and puffy eyes ruin her masterpiece before we even start."

"Speaking of masterpieces," Brenna pulled out a chair at the kitchen table and patted it expectantly. "Sit. We have work to do."

"You don't have to do this," I said, even as I was already moving toward the chair. "I'm capable of getting ready by myself."

"Of course you are," Sorcha agreed. "But why would you want to deny the two of us our fun?"

They leaned their heads together and grinned.

I rolled my eyes, settled into the chair, and immediately felt Sorcha's fingers in my hair, sectioning and testing different arrangements. It was soothing in a way I had a hard time admitting I enjoyed—being cared for like this, fussed over.

"Nervous?" Brenna asked, unpacking what seemed like an entire shop's worth of cosmetics.

"A little," I admitted. "Good, nervous, though. More like... this-is-really-happening nervous."

"It's really happening," Sorcha confirmed, beginning to braid. "In a few hours, you'll be officially bound to that gorgeous male who's been following you around like a lovesick puppy for months."

"He doesn't follow me around," I protested.

"Meira," Brenna said flatly. "The male changed his entire work schedule so he could work on wards whenever you were."

"Plus," Sorcha added, tugging gently on a section of hair, "Conor told me Calder didn't shut up about you the entire time he visited his workshop yesterday. Apparently he tried to start three different projects and couldn't concentrate on any of them."

I liked the image of him nervous and restless. "Really?"

"Really. You're both complete disasters, and it's the most romantic thing I've ever seen."

I let them work, chattering about the ceremony and the festival, about how beautiful the meadow would look in the golden hour light. My nerves finally settled into anticipation mixed with joy.

"First things first," Brenna said, surveying my face. "You need food."

"I'm not really hungry," I said, which was true. My stomach was too full of butterflies to make room for actual food.

"That's what everyone says right before they faint at the

altar," Sorcha said firmly, already moving toward my stove. "I'm making eggs. You're eating them."

While Sorcha cooked, Brenna started working on my hair alongside Sorcha's braiding, and the cottage filled with the warm, familiar chaos of my best friends taking care of me. It reminded me of childhood mornings when we'd get ready for festivals together, except this time felt infinitely more important.

"Tell me honestly," I said as Sorcha worked another intricate twist into my hair, "what if I'm rushing into this? What if we're better as friends than as... whatever this is? Am I crazy for doing this so fast?"

"You mean binding yourself to someone you've been in love with for months?" Brenna asked, carefully applying something that made my eyes look wider. "Some people spend years trying to find what you two have stumbled into."

"You've known him for two years. It's not like you're marrying a stranger," Sorcha added.

"Plus," Brenna added, "I've never seen you this happy. Not once in all the years I've known you."

"Eat," Sorcha commanded, setting a plate of perfectly scrambled eggs in front of me.

I managed several bites, more to appease them than because I had any appetite and surprisingly, the warmth of the food helped quiet some of the butterflies.

Time moved strangely as they worked their magic. Sorcha's fingers wove flowers through elaborate braids that transformed my hair into something fit for ancient stories. Brenna worked magic on my face, somehow making my cheekbones more defined and my lips look fuller without making me look like someone else entirely.

They chattered constantly, filling the cottage with laughter and speculation about who would be at the festival, whether old Hamish would cry during the ceremony (he always did), and how scandalized Mrs. Blackwood would be when she saw how handsome Calder looked in formal clothes.

"Speaking of which," Brenna said, stepping back to admire her work, "we should probably get you into that dress soon. We'll have to leave soon."

My heart jumped. "Already?"

"Ready?" Sorcha asked, lifting the dress carefully above my head.

The dress fit like it had been made for me, draped and flowing in soft waves over every curve. The embroidery Sorcha had added made it feel both elegant and personal, like something my mother might have worn.

"Oh," I breathed, catching sight of myself in the mirror. "Oh, Sorcha."

"Don't you dare cry," she warned, but her own eyes were suspiciously bright. "You look perfect."

"One more thing," Brenna said, unfastening a bracelet from her own wrist—delicate silver links that caught the light. "My mother gave this to me on my sixteenth birthday. Something borrowed." She clasped it around my wrist, and the weight of it felt like a blessing.

"Now you're perfect," Sorcha declared.

The walk to the meadow felt both endless and far too short.

Lughnasadh had transformed the meadow into something magical. Bundles of late-harvest grain and woven corn dollies adorned every post and tree, while tended bonfires crackled in carefully placed circles, dancing shadows across the gathering crowd. Musicians played near the trees, and children ran between the adults with flowers in their hair, their laughter bright as bells.

But all I could see was the ceremonial circle at the center of it all, where Elder Muriel waited with the binding cords draped over her arms. And there, standing with his back to us, hands clasped behind him, was Calder.

He was already there, of course he was. He wore deep forest green that brought out the gold in his eyes, his hair was half-pulled back like always, a few braids tucked in, the rest loose around his shoulders. Even from behind, I could see the tension in his posture. It was the same nervous energy I'd been carrying all day.

As if he sensed me approaching, he turned, and the world narrowed to just his face. His eyes widened as his gaze moved over me slowly as he took in the dress, the flowers, my hair.

Then his face broke into a smile so bright, I had no choice but to match it.

He walked toward me, and the crowd parted without him even seeming to notice. When he reached me, he stopped just close enough that I caught his familiar scent, could see the way his hands trembled slightly at his sides.

"You look..." he started, then seemed to lose his words entirely.

"You're not too bad yourself," I said, reaching up to straighten his collar just because I needed to touch him.

His hand covered mine against his chest, where his heart hammered beneath my palm. "I've been here for hours," he admitted. "Couldn't concentrate on anything else."

"How many?"

"Two," he said with a crooked grin. "Conor finally said we just had to leave because I was driving him crazy."

Elder Muriel cleared her throat gently. "Shall we begin?"

The ceremony itself was simple and traditional, but every word felt weighted. We stood facing each other while Muriel spoke about binding and choosing, about the sacred nature of partnership. But I could barely hear her. The only thing I knew was Calder's face, the way he looked at me, the careful way he reached for my hands when Muriel told us to join them.

His hands were warm and steady, real and solid. He was here, this was happening.

"Do you have words you'd like to speak to each other?" Muriel asked.

Calder nodded and reached into his pocket, pulling out a folded piece of paper. His hands shook slightly as he opened it, and when he began to read, his voice was rough.

"Meira," he began, then had to clear his throat and start again. "When I came to this valley, I thought I was looking for a purpose. For somewhere to belong. For work that mattered." He paused, looking directly at me. "I found all of that. But what I didn't expect to find was home."

Everything inside me went soft at once.

"You told me once that your father believed he and your mother were made from the same handful of stardust. That their bones remembered it." His voice grew stronger, more certain. "I've never stopped thinking about that. Because being with you has always felt like coming home. Something in me has always remembered you."

Tears slipped down my cheeks before I could stop them.

"You are my home, Meira. My purpose. My recognition." His thumbs brushed over my knuckles. "And if there's any truth in what your father believed— then I think we were made from the same dust too."

"Meira?" Elder Muriel prompted gently, her voice seemed to be very far away.

I hadn't prepared anything. I hadn't even thought about writing vows. But looking at Calder, seeing the love written across his face, the words came anyway.

"I spent my whole life watching the kind of love that made everything feel magical," I began, my voice shaking. "The way my parents could make even the simplest moments—sharing tea, working in the garden—feel like enough, like everything."

I pressed my lips together, holding everything in place, and

Calder's thumb rubbed encouraging circles over the backs of my hands.

"I didn't think I'd have that. I convinced myself I didn't need it, that I've always been just fine on my own." I looked at him, and the words came easier. "But you... you make it impossible to remember how that felt. You showed me that loving you didn't mean losing myself." I took a deep breath and tried to memorize every part of this moment.

"I realized I've spent a lot of time just getting by, but you make even mundane moments feel touched by wonder. You make me feel worthy of love—not because of what I do or how useful I am, but just because I exist."

The words tumbled out of me now, "With you, there's all kinds of magic hidden in ordinary things."

Calder's eyes were bright with unshed tears.

He reached for me before the last words had settled, his hands cradling my face with his familiar gentleness. He leaned down until our foreheads touched, and I could feel his smile against my skin.

"*You* are the magic, Meira," he whispered back. "You always have been."

Elder Muriel began binding our hands with the ceremonial cord, wrapping it around our joined wrists in the traditional pattern. The rope was soft, worn smooth by countless ceremonies before ours, but it felt like the most important thing in the world.

"By the laws ancient and new, witnessed by your friends in this community and blessed by the gods," she announced, "you are bound in intention and promise. May your hearts remember what your hands have sworn."

The crowd erupted in cheers, but Calder and I stayed frozen, staring at each other with wonder. Our hands were bound, our vows spoken, our love declared before everyone who mattered.

He was mine, and I was his. The thought sent a thrill through me so sharp it was almost painful.

"Kiss her, you idiot!" Conor's voice rang out, unmistakable. Calder laughed, the sound bright and free.

"Gladly," he murmured, and kissed me like we were the only two people in the world.

24

———

I opened my mother's recipe book to the page with the folded corner, the parchment thin and yellowed with age. This was one of the few things I'd refused to part with after she died. I'd never actually cooked from it with her, but this page was covered in her handwriting—those familiar loops and swirls in faded ink that still made my chest ache.

These were the scones she made every solstice morning.

I wanted to make them with honey and lavender, the way Calder had mentioned his mother used to. This mattered too much to mess up, so I'd begged Aoife to help me adapt the recipe. Something from his mother, something from mine.

I poured the measured flour into the bowl, a small cloud of white powder billowing upward. A few specks missed the bowl entirely, landing on an impatient and curious Kit, who violently sneezed several times, her tiny nose twitching.

"Goodness," I laughed, as she scratched at her nose with a delicate paw. The sound of my own laughter still surprised me sometimes—how long had it been since I'd laughed so freely so often, without the weight of the wards pressing down on me?

Calder had gone to check them all this morning alone. He'd

been insistent, promising there had been nothing wrong in weeks. "Sleep in," he'd murmured against my temple last night, his large hand splayed protectively across my abdomen. "Just this once."

Unfortunately, my body didn't know how to sleep past dawn anymore. Years of ward duty had trained it too well. But I'd pretended to be asleep when he rose this morning, keeping my breathing even, just so I could hear him whisper that he loved me before he pressed his lips to my forehead.

There hadn't been a morning since our handfasting that we hadn't spent together, bodies entwined beneath the quilts. I loved waking up to him, usually with his bare chest pressed against my back, his warmth chasing away the morning chill. He was his own source of heat, my personal hearth.

I slipped the scones into the oven, set a timer, and washed the dishes quickly. I didn't want to ruin the surprise before they were finished. Just as I put the mixing bowl away, I heard the back door creak open. I winked at Kit, my sleepy little co-conspirator. She was usually glued to Calder's heels, but she wasn't much for getting out of bed before sunrise.

He carried my mother's old harvesting basket, the one we used to collect things from the garden that had once been hers. I'd once thought I'd never feel close to my parents again, but having her things here, using her spaces, watching Calder step so naturally into the patterns my father had once filled—it brought me an indescribable comfort.

He'd picked the season's last peppers, pulled carrots and potatoes dusted with rich black soil, snipped a few sprigs of fragrant rosemary, and cut a handful of roses, huge blooms with layer upon layer of velvety petals.

"Hi," he said with a smile that still made my magic stir beneath my skin. He kissed the top of my head as he passed, and still, somehow, that one kiss warmed my insides.

I watched him trim the rose stems with his knife, those big

hands unexpectedly gentle with the delicate blooms. I pulled out a vase without being asked, filled it with water. It still amazed me, having someone who thought of me like this. Those flowers would have been just as beautiful staying on the bush outside, but Calder couldn't seem to help himself. Fresh flowers inside, always.

He'd told me once that his mother and Sylvie had loved having fresh flowers in the house, cutting them together to fill every room with color. I understood now that each bloom he brought inside was a way of remembering them, of keeping their love for beauty alive in the life we were building together.

The recipe book was still open by the stove. I snapped it shut, the sound making Calder glance back with curiosity. I ducked my head, suddenly fascinated by an already-spotless counter.

He arranged the roses in the vase with the same careful attention he gave everything.

"Do you want some tea?" he asked, filling the kettle with water.

"Sure," I said, but I'd said it too quickly and sounded sharp.

He paused, but didn't question me. I brushed away nonexistent flour from the counters, wiped the spot where Kit had sneezed earlier, unable to keep my hands still.

"The wards looked perfect this morning," he offered, setting the kettle on the stove.

"Hmm," was all I managed in response.

I opened the towel drawer and pulled out every tea towel, just to refold them with unnecessary precision. I could feel him watching me, patient as always.

"I think the wards look just as good as yesterday," he continued conversationally. "The living connections haven't needed anything at all in days. They're going to change everything." A pause. "For both of us."

He was trying to draw me out, I could tell. Baiting me with

ward talk, knowing how it usually worked. But today, the wards were the furthest thing from my mind.

"You okay?" The concern in his voice made me look up.

"I'm fine," I said automatically. The response was so practiced it slipped out before I could stop it. I'd been trying to break that habit, to actually tell him how I felt instead of defaulting to fine.

I caught myself wiping the table for the third time since he'd returned, his watchful gaze following my movements.

I caught myself wiping the same spot on the table for the third time, his eyes tracking my nervous movements.

"Meira." His voice carried gentle authority, the kind that made me finally meet his gaze. I tried to look innocent, though my heart was hammering.

"What's wrong?" he pressed.

"Nothing," I said immediately.

The timer saved me, its shrill ring cutting through the tension. I lunged for the oven, but Calder was faster, his long legs carrying him there before me. He blocked the oven door with his body, a mountain I couldn't move.

I reached around him, but he caught my wrist, his grip gentle but immovable. His other hand tilted my chin up until I had no choice but to look at him. The tenderness in his eyes made my chest ache. I'd never imagined anyone would look at me like that. It was the way Conor looked at Sorcha, the way my father had looked at my mother.

"Meira," he said again, my name soft on his lips.

I gave up fighting. "What?"

"Tell me what's wrong." His thumb brushed my cheek, and I could see him starting to panic. "You're scaring me."

"I really need to get those out of the oven," I insisted, my voice barely above a whisper.

He searched my face for another heartbeat before stepping

aside and releasing his hold. I grabbed oven mitts and pulled out the scones, which were—to put it kindly, hideous.

Lumpy, lopsided things that had expanded in completely wrong directions. But they smelled incredible, honey and lavender filling the kitchen.

"They're scones," I said weakly, setting the tray down. "Or they were supposed to be."

Calder stared at them, his brow furrowed. I could practically see him trying to find something honest but kind to say.

"They're ugly," I said, laughing nervously. "You can say it."

His face broke into that smile that crinkled his eyes. "They're a bit..."

"Ugly," I supplied.

"But they smell amazing," he finished quickly.

I hoped to all the ancient gods that they tasted better than they looked. I transferred a couple to a plate and set them beside his tea mug. My fingers twisting the fabric of my apron.

"Meira, what's going on?" The worry was back, shadowing his features. "Are you—" He looked at the scones, then at me, and genuine alarm flashed across his face. "These aren't...are these break-up scones?"

My magic flared in protest, golden light dancing over my fingertips. "Calder, no. Gods, no."

"Then what—"

"Eat the scone, Calder," I commanded, pointing to his plate. The tension in my voice belied the lightness I was attempting.

His eyes narrowed, but I caught him fighting a smile. The corner of his mouth twitched. Good, we were flirting now, back to familiar territory.

He picked up a scone, examining it with exaggerated suspicion, turning it over in his large hands. "Calder. Eat it," I insisted, crossing my arms.

He took a cautious bite, his eyes never leaving mine. Then he looked back at the scone, then to me, then back to the scone again. His second bite was bigger, followed by a low sound of appreciation that sent heat straight through me.

"Meira," he said, wonder creeping into his voice. "These taste just like my mother's."

"Really?" Hope soared in my chest. "I got it right?"

"I mean, I never would have told her this, but..." His smile went soft with memory. "They're almost exactly the same."

Relief flooded through me. All of it—the anxiety, the early morning baking, the mess—had been worth it.

Then I remembered why I'd made them in the first place, and my courage faltered. "Calder, I—"

"You said these weren't break-up scones," he interrupted, his tone half-joking but with an undercurrent of concern.

I laughed nervously, picking at the fraying hem of my apron. "They're not break-up scones."

"Then what's happening, Meira? Are you... are you sick? Dying?" His expression had gone serious again, worry etching lines between his brows.

I closed my eyes and shook my head, amazed at where his mind went when panicked. "They're move-in scones."

He stopped mid-chew, eyes widening. I watched his pupils dilate as understanding hit. "Move-in scones?" he repeated carefully, like he might have misheard.

I blew out a breath and threw my hands up in exasperation. Why was this so hard? This male that I loved beyond anything I thought possible, this person who had become my entire world, who had shown me that duty and joy weren't mutually exclusive—he was watching me with such hope that my chest physically ached with the weight of it.

"They're move-in scones," I confirmed, my voice steadier now. "I wanted to ask you if you'd like to move in with me. Here. Permanently."

He shot to his feet so fast his chair nearly toppled, closing the distance between us in a single stride. His hand cupped my face, tilting it up. "Do you mean it?" His voice was rough with emotion.

I nodded, laughing and crying at the same time. A tear escaped, and he kissed it away before lifting me off my feet, spinning me around the kitchen.

"Move-in scones?" Joy made him sound almost boyish. "You want me to live here?"

"I want you here always," I said, looking down at him from my elevated position. "Not just mornings, not just when we check the wards, not just the nights you stay over. I want this to be your home."

He tipped his face up, and I leaned down to meet him. Our kiss tasted like honey and lavender, like everything sweet I'd ever wanted. We were laughing and kissing and crying all at once, emotion and magic tangling together.

"Then I'm yours," he said against my lips. "Whatever comes next, I'm yours."

I melted into him completely, wrapping my legs around his waist. His hands gripped my hips, holding me steady.

"Want to see your new bedroom?" I whispered against his ear, letting my lips brush the sensitive skin. Goosebumps erupted across his neck, and when I nipped his earlobe, he shuddered.

"Do I get a dresser drawer?" he teased, voice husky, already carrying me toward the bedroom.

I laughed, even as heat pooled low in my belly.

"What about my things? I have a few pairs of boots, and the trunk with my—"

"Calder," I interrupted, "you can have whatever you want, but if you don't make love to me right now, I might actually die."

He growled—a sound that vibrated through his chest into mine—and claimed my mouth again. Within seconds we were a tangle of limbs and skin under the covers, moving together with desperate need.

Whatever forces moved in this world, whatever the fae were made of, whatever enchantment wove through the very fabric of our existence, this extraordinary thing between us was the purest magic of all.

After, we lay with nothing to do and nowhere to be. He sprawled on his back, one arm behind his head, the other around me as I draped myself over him, tracing lazy patterns on his chest.

He played with my hair, winding strands around his fingers. I gazed up at him, memorizing the happiness on his face, his eyes closed but his lips curved in a soft smile.

"Calder," I said softly.

"Mmm?" The contentment in his voice matched his expression, making me smile.

"I want you to take me somewhere." The words came out quietly, but sure. "Somewhere far from here. Just the two of us."

His eyes fluttered open, bright with wonder.

"Anywhere you want to go," he said.

I settled back against his chest, already dreaming. "Tell me about that castle again. The one by the sea."

ABOUT THE AUTHOR

Olivia McCullough writes fantasy romance from her Midwest home, where she lives with her husband and son. A marketing consultant by day and writer by night, she dreams of trading tornado seasons for Scottish highlands. *The Hidden Magic of Ordinary Things* is her debut novel.

For bonus content and updates on future books, visit olivi amccullough.com.